A Good Old Fashioned Redneck Country Christmas: The Musical

by Kris Bauske

Additional Music Contributions
by Brent Bauske

A SAMUEL FRENCH ACTING EDITION

FOUNDED 1830

NEW YORK HOLLYWOOD LONDON TORONTO

SAMUELFRENCH.COM

ISBN 978-0-573-69922-1   Printed in U.S.A.   #29863

RENTAL MATERIALS

An orchestration consisting of **Piano/Vocal Score** will be loaned two months prior to the production ONLY on the receipt of the Licensing Fee quoted for all performances, the rental fee and a refundable deposit.

Please contact Samuel French for perusal of the music materials as well as a performance license application.

IMPORTANT BILLING AND CREDIT
REQUIREMENTS

All producers of *A GOOD, OLD FASHIONED, REDNECK COUNTRY CHRISTMAS must* give credit to the Author of the Play in all programs distributed in connection with performances of the Play, and in all instances in which the title of the Play appears for the purposes of advertising, publicizing or otherwise exploiting the Play and/or a production. The name of the Author *must* appear on a separate line on which no other name appears, immediately following the title and *must* appear in size of type not less than fifty percent of the size of the title type.

The Osceola Center for the Arts hosted the professional debut of *A GOOD OLD FASHIONED REDNECK COUNTRY CHRISTMAS: THE MUSICAL* on July 31, 2010. Produced and directed by Kris Bauske. This production would not have been possible without the generous support of Arin Gullett and Ed C. Moore at OCFTA. Thank you! The cast (in order of appearance) was as follows:

NARRATOR.....................................Duane Fioravanti
CHARLIE ....Brent Bauske
LOU WEXLER ....Gail Golden
BARBIE JO FOX ....Eve Meilke
DARLENE FULMAN ....Drea Monzon
DAVE FOX...Scott Sheplee
JIMMY WEAVER.....................................Jim Pollard
BILL WEXLER....................................Shawn Kilgore
MARK RILEY......................................John (JT) Diaz
MARY SUE ARCHER ....Bella Muller

CHARACTERS

LOU (LOUISE) WEXLER – Lou is a bubbling bundle of energy. She takes command of the stage like she takes command of her diner. Mid 30s, she is attractive, intelligent, and well-respected. Both men and women find value in Lou's many philosophies of life. She has a feminine build with a generous bust line. She would never be considered thin, but she's not fat either, and she's proud of her womanly curves. Her hair and make-up are flawless, and she exudes an air of utter capability. Lou is always moving, and dispensing tough, no-nonsense wisdom as she bounces from one task to another throughout the diner she's owned and loved since she was in her early 20s. Perhaps the only empty place in Lou's life comes from the fact that she and her husband, Bill, have not conceived a child of their own. She is ready to adopt, but Bill isn't so sure. Lou is energetic hospitality personified. She speaks with a slight southern drawl which is warm and welcoming – never hillbilly harsh.

BILL WEXLER – Bill is a retired marine who served in the First Gulf War and is married to Lou. Mid to late 30s, he is taller than the other men, wears his hair in a typical military style, and has an air of authority that is impossible to miss. He owns a trail guiding business, and his physique indicates his athleticism. He grew up in the town of Christmas and loves hiking, fishing, and hunting. He speaks with the same warm, southern drawl that Lou uses. Bill personifies male leadership, but he is conflicted over whether he and Lou should change their lives and become parents. If any of the men understand women and relationships, Bill's the man. Bill doesn't take orders from the boys, but his philosophy concerning women is generally to do as Lou says.

DAVE FOX – Dave is a typical, married father of two in his 30s who just happens to speak with a southern drawl and work as a butcher. He is painfully average in looks and intelligence. Dave cultivated his great sense of humor to compensate for his overly average averageness. He loves to crack jokes to avoid any real discussion of issues. Way down deep inside, he loves his wife and children, but he feels that his mother-in-law is just too much to deal with at Christmas. Dave and Bill have been friends all their lives, and Jimmy is the butt of many of Dave's jokes because Dave secretly envies Jimmy's free and easy bachelor life.

BARBIE JO FOX – Barbie Jo is the beleaguered wife of Dave and the daughter of Verna Belle. She has two children and Dave to raise. She is attractive but frazzled. She never quite manages to look completely put together. Barbie Jo's mother never lets her forget that she could have married better, gotten a better education, and just generally done better in life if she hadn't married Dave the butcher right out of high school. Barbie Jo works full-time at the diner, and Lou considers Barbie Jo her 'right hand girl'. Barbie Jo's trying to make everybody happy for Christmas and succeeding with no one. Speaks with warm, southern accent.

JIMMY WEAVER – Jimmy considers himself the 'lady's man' in town. In his mid 20s, he is cute and charming, but he isn't terribly smart. He is woefully lacking in any understanding of what women really want from a man. Jimmy's family has owned a hog farm near town for generations, and Jimmy is a real, down-home, farm boy. He loves to hunt and fish and basically do whatever he darn well pleases. He is dating the town hottie, Darlene, but he isn't interested in marriage, just yet. He loves Darlene, but he's not ready to give up his bachelor life, if only to make Bill and Dave jealous. He met Bill and Lou when he started dating Darlene, and Bill and Dave added him to their group right away because he shares their love of women, beer, and most of all, hunting! Jimmy speaks with a distinct southern drawl.

DARLENE FULMER – Darlene is the lollipop under the Christmas tree! In her early 20s, she is blonde and built! Darlene wears short skirts and tight sweaters. She is a typical rodeo queen with horses on her mind and cowboys on her tail. No hairstyle is too big, no jewelry too outrageous for Darlene. She is a complete innocent who accepts everything at face value. No one considers Darlene a brain, but what she lacks in smarts, she makes up for in heart. She met Jimmy through an internet dating service two years ago because she was tired of meeting men who just 'wanted her for her body'. Darlene is ready to move on to the next step in their relationship, but Jimmy is happy with the way things are. She is a horrible singer, but loves to sing! She loves everything to do with Christmas! Darlene is a good hearted gal who just wants to make the world a better place! Speaks with the southern drawl typical of all Christmas residents.

BOB/NARRATOR – Bob is a truck driver in his 50s or 60s who is also a road warrior/philosopher. He taught high school English before retiring to go on the road. Bob loves his wife and family and is not happy to be stranded away from them on Christmas Eve, but he's wise enough to know that he can't change his circumstances. He sees every obstacle as a new challenge and an opportunity to observe people. He loves to read the classics and writes and ruminates about the people he meets on the road. Bob may speak with or without a southern drawl.

MARY SUE ARCHER – Mary Sue is the unwitting 'gift of Christmas'. She is a young woman in her late teens or early 20s who arrives in town on the evening bus. Everything she owns, she carries in a satchel at her side. Her second-hand coat cannot close over the huge bump of her pregnant belly. She wears serviceable snow boots, a knit hat, and a long, shabby scarf. Mary Sue has long, dark hair, and she speaks with a southern drawl. She is alone in the world and looks lost and desolate. She is used to being ignored and is surprised when Lou and the girls take an interest in her welfare. Even though she has been discarded by her family, Mary Sue still believes there is inherent goodness in people, and she has hope for a better future for her baby.

MARK RILEY – Mark is a twenty year-old, first year medical student and the only son of the town doctor. He is currently attending medical school himself. Mark is young, thin, and not-quite handsome, and he is devoted to medicine. Mark always wears his glasses and has his nose buried in his books. Mark is considered a loveable, brainy geek by the residents of Christmas. He has never dated, but he's always had a secret crush on Darlene. Mark is home from college for the Christmas break. He speaks with a southern drawl as well, but it need not be as pronounced as the others.

CHARLIE REYNOLDS – A man from 30 to 60. Charlie is the town banker and may be wearing a nice suit and overcoat or blue jeans and a heavy parka. After all, it's Christmas Eve! He is definitely bundled up for bad weather! A quick walk-on role to get things going. Charlie and Lou are old friends. Charlie may be doubled by either Jimmy or Dave, but if the director makes this choice, please have the actor wear the suit and overcoat, and maybe a fake mustache and/or glasses to throw the audience off the track.

SETTING

There is one basic set divided into three sections.

The Diner – Lou's Diner is a typical small town diner. There are booths and tables on the checkerboard floor. Chrome tables and chairs hailing from the fifties era give the diner the air of authentic nostalgia. The booths run along the front window of the diner. A counter sits at the back of the diner set, and a door next to the counter and a window behind it are open into the kitchen area. There is a coat rack in the corner near the front door. A large, cheery cow bell hangs from the door that rings when the door is opened or closed. There are menus in a stack on the counter next to a pile of silverware wrapped in napkins. Napkin dispensers, plastic holders for small containers of cream and jelly, and salt and pepper shakers sit on each table. Every detail is authentic.

The diner is decorated for Christmas. Gold garland hangs at the large picture window with small silver balls hanging from the loops in the garland. Christmas decorations nearly obscure the view through the picture window. A picture of Santa Claus is affixed to the front of the counter, and more garland is strung around the window to the kitchen. Mistletoe hangs over the door. A lighted Christmas tree sits near the window. The tree is almost completely decorated. An angel sits atop the tree. Falling snow is visible through the window.

The Cabin – The hunting cabin is rough and woodsy. There is an exterior door at the back of the cabin and a window off to one side. There are no curtains on the window. This is a manly man's cabin. Falling snow is visible through the window.

A bar with two bar stools sits in front of the window. There is a sofa in the center of the room with an old chair off to one side. The arm of the chair appears to have been broken at some point and repaired with duct tape. A hand crocheted afghan is tossed carelessly over the back of the sofa. An ottoman rests in front of the chair, and a coffee table sits before the sofa. None of these items match, as if placed there more for comfort and usefulness than for appearance. A worn room rug is on the floor under the coffee table.

A large moose head hangs on the wall above the door. The cabin is wood paneled and sparse. A cooler sits on the floor between the chair and the sofa. A bag of groceries (unhealthy snack foods) sits on the bar. An unused wood stove is near the wall, and the wood box is nearly empty.

The Woods – The woods are dense and covered in snow. Heavy snow falls and blows from all directions. The wind howls. This is a blizzard!

The Animal Shed – The Diner is transformed into the Animal Shed during the last scene. There is an exterior door and three stalls with swinging doors on the front of each. All wood in the animal shed is old and rough. It has weathered many winters just like this one. The door to the middle stall opens out toward the exterior door to the shed. This initially obscures the view that the women have of Mary Sue and the baby when they enter and must be set up this way.

Bales of hay sit in front of one stall. (If available, a cow or donkey stands in this stall.) A closet with saddles, bridles, lead ropes, and blankets is on the side of the stage farthest from the front door. A chest holding barn items such as hoof pick and bag balm is on a bale of hay near the door.

The floor of the center stall, like the rest of the animal shed, is covered with loose hay, and there are bales of hay in the center stall as well. The final stall is in the corner, and the wall in the corner is cracked. Snow occasionally blows in through the damaged area. A two by four sits in the corner to hold up the dilapidated tin roof. Bales of hay are piled higher in the third stall. A discarded saddle blanket lies over the top rail of the third stall.

LIGHTING

To facilitate the smooth transition from one scene to the next, it is necessary to cross-fade lights between scenes. Never go to black.

An adjustable spot is required on Mary Sue during the nativity scene with the light gradually becoming more intense as the music swells and then gradually dimming again to normal. A star can be shone on the wall above the animal shed if available, or through the gaping hole in the roof.

A scrim is used during Act II, Scene Three to create the silhouettes of The Three Wise Men.

AUTHOR'S NOTES

This play is written for a two act performance. However, if the director wishes to run the play straight through, he or she is welcome to do so.

SCENES AND MUSICAL NUMBERS

ACT ONE

Scene 1   Lou's Diner

"Christmas in the Country". . . . . **BOB**

"I'm a Kiwi" . . . .**LOU & BARBIE JO**

Scene 2   The Interior of the Hunting Cabin

"Beehive" . . . .**DAVE, JIMMY, AND BILL**

Scene 3   Lou's Diner

"Cattin' Around:. . . . . **DARLENE, LOU & BARBIE JO**

"Mary, Mary". . . . . **DARLENE, LOU & BARBIE JO**

ACT TWO

Scene 1   The Winter Woods

Scene 2   The Interior of the Hunting Cabin

"We are Men!". . . . . **DAVE, JIMMY, AND BILL**

Scene 3   The Wilson's Animal Shed

"Snowy Christmas Day" . . . .**MARK**

Scene 4   The Wilson's Animal Shed

"A Good, Old Fashioned, Redneck Country Christmas" . . . .**ALL**

ACT I

Scene One

(AT RISE: Inside Lou's Diner. This is any small town diner in the mountains of the south: West Virginia, Tennessee, Kentucky, etc. Not fancy, but not dirty either. **LOU** *is an energetic, no-nonsense woman who runs a clean place and dispenses wisdom and advice along with the best food in town. The front door is upstage right. To the rear is a counter with stools. Behind the counter is a serving window that reveals the kitchen. Stage right has a large plate glass window with decorations around it and a large Christmas tree in front of it. Three oak tables with three chairs each are scattered around the restaurant.)*

*(***BOB/NARRATOR*** stands beside the window. He is a customer and is always part of the restaurant atmosphere. Behind him, frozen in mid-action are* **LOU,** **CHARLIE, BARBIE JO,** *and* **DARLENE.** **MARK** *sits frozen at a separate table, deep in his studies.)*

BOB/NARRATOR. Well, howdy folks! I'm glad y'all made it safe and sound. That snow had me worried. Sure is pilin' up out there. But snow's part of any Christmas story, and that's what this is – a Christmas story. Confidentially, the whole dadburned thing is so amazin', you're gonna think I made it up!

(pause)

It all started when my truck broke down and I ended up here in Lou's Diner waitin' on Travis Hawkins to fix her up. It's Christmas Eve. Can you see the snow fallin' outside that window? Now I know what you must be thinkin'. You're thinkin', he can't see out that window. There's too many decorations in the way! But I can see way beyond that window.

11

BOB/NARRATOR. *(cont.)* Out there is the town of Christmas. Rows of small houses all decorated with lights. Snowmen on the lawns. An old barn sitting on a small rise beside the icehouse road. A small peaked roof with a weather vane. And a big old Prince Albert Tobacco sign tucked just beside the Baptist church.

(The bell rings as **CHARLIE** *enters the diner. Lights come up on* **LOU**.*)*

LOU. Hiya, Charlie! Got your stuff here. How's Donna?

CHARLIE. She's practicing for the Christmas program tonight.

LOU. She doing 'Away in a Manger?' It's my favorite, you know.

CHARLIE. Yep. Just for you, Lou. A little 'Thank You' for the pies. Gives her more time to practice.

LOU. My pleasure, Charlie! Happy to help.

*(***LOU*** *takes money from* **CHARLIE** *who carries a large paper bag with bundles with "Lou's Diner" printed on the side. He also picks up a white bakery box tied with string as he prpares to leave.)*

CHARLIE. Happy Holidays!

LOU. Charlie! You know in my place, there's a standing rule – it's always 'Merry Christmas' at Lou's Diner!

CHARLIE. Merry Christmas, Lou!

(exits and bell rings on door)

*(***LOU***,* **BARBIE JO**, *and* **DARLENE** *freeze as* **BOB** *sings.)*

BOB/NARRATOR. Nice folks! Some might say 'old fashioned', but seems this little town is just full of good, country people! Reminds me of Christmas as a boy...

(Music starts as **BOB** *speaks the first two verses. Lights come up on* **BOB**. **LOU** *freezes behind him.)*

CHRISTMAS IN THE COUNTRY - BOB

BOB. *(speaks)* I'm lookin' at a picture
    Straight from Currier and Ives
    And these are the happy days
    We'll think of all our lives

    Remembering traditions
    I learned at Grand Dads's knee
    Like these folks, he felt there's ways
    Things always ought to be.

    (sings)

    CHRISTMAS IN THE COUNTRY
    SMELL THE PUMPKIN PIES
    CHESTNUTS ON THE FIRE
    LET'S SEE THOSE REINDEER FLY!
    HAPPY SLEIGH BELLS RINGING
    IN A WONDERLAND OF WHITE
    CAROLERS A SINGING
    EVERYTHING SEEMS RIGHT!

    HOLD ON TO TRADITIONS,
    MEAN THE WORDS YOU SAY,
    GENERATIONS FOLLOWING
    WILL HAVE A DEBT TO PAY.

    SHARE A HAPPY GREETING!
    IT'S MORE THAN JUST A PHRASE.
    HAVE A MERRY CHRISTMAS
    NOT 'HAPPY HOLIDAYS'!

    CHRISTMAS IN THE COUNTRY
    IT'S FROSTY IN THE SNOW
    SANTA CLAUS IS COMING,
    ASK ANY KID YOU KNOW

    THE SNOW KEEPS FALLIN' ROUND US
    THE KETTLE'S ON THE FIRE
    I WOULDN'T EVEN BE HERE
    IF I HADN'T BLOWN A TIRE!

BOB. *(cont.)*

HOLD ON TO TRADITIONS,
MEAN THE WORDS YOU SAY,
GENERATIONS FOLLOWING
WILL HAVE A DEBT TO PAY.

SHARE A HAPPY GREETING!
IT'S MORE THAN JUST A PHRASE.
HAVE A MERRY CHRISTMAS
NOT 'HAPPY HOLIDAYS'!

CHRISTMAS IN THE COUNTRY
SEE THE CHRISTMAS TREE
HANGING UP THE GARLAND
BUT YOU'RE NOT HERE WITH ME.

I'LL BE HOME FOR CHRISTMAS,
THIS I SWEAR TO YOU.
AND IF I CANNOT MAKE IT
I'LL MAKE IT UP TO YOU!
HOLD ON TO TRADITIONS,
MEAN THE WORDS YOU SAY,
GENERATIONS FOLLOWING
WILL HAVE A DEBT TO PAY.

SHARE A HAPPY GREETING!
IT'S MORE THAN JUST A PHRASE.
HAVE A MERRY CHRISTMAS
NOT 'HAPPY HOLIDAYS'!

JINGLE BELLS, JINGLE BELLS,
THEY JINGLE ALL THE WAY
HAVE A MERRY CHRISTMAS
NOT 'HAPPY HOLIDAYS'!

HAVE A MERRY CHRISTMAS!
NOT 'HAPPY HOLIDAYS'!

Folks, if you ever want a real-life education, plop yourself down here in Lou's Diner. You'll find three of the feistiest gals you're ever gonna meet! As for the men in their lives, well, heck, they high tailed it outta here. Went huntin's what they did – on Christmas Eve! Caused quite a stink around here, let me tell you.

(Suddenly the diner comes alive. **LOU** *is cleaning silverware,* **DARLENE** *wears an elf costume with a mini skirt and bells on her turned up toes. She is fussing with the Christmas tree.* **MARK** *absent-mindedly turns a page in his giant book and sips his coffee.* **BARBIE JO** *is nervously pacing up and down, talking to her mother on her cell phone.* **BOB/NARRATOR** *observes as he returns to his table and sits.)*

DARLENE. *(sings)*

OH CHRISTMAS TREE, OH CHRISTMAS TREE, HOW LOVELY ARE THY BRANCHES. OH CHRISTMAS TREE, OH!

(looks out window)

Oh look! It's starting to snow!

(claps hands and bounces up and down)

DARLENE. *(cont.)* I love snow! Snow is the prettiest, sparkliest, most amazing part of Christmas! I love snow more than anything in the whole world!

LOU. Darlene, stop your yapping and get Bob another cup of coffee. Does Mark need anything?

DARLENE. *(looks at* **MARK** *who concentrates on his book)* I don't think Mark even know he's here.

MARK. What? What's that, Darlene?

DARLENE. So you are here!

MARK. Of course I am! Where else would I be? Did you need something, Darlene?

DARLENE. I was just fixin' to ask you the same thing, Mark!

MARK. You sure look pretty today, Darlene! Course, you look pretty every day!

DARLENE. What? This old thing?

MARK. You could be one of Santa's elves!

DARLENE. That's where I got the outfit! I was an elf at Whitman's store a few years back, and old Mr. Whitman insisted on having it made for me!

MARK. You don't do that any more?

DARLENE. I quit when Santa spent as much time trying to get me on his lap as he did the kids! It was wreckin' my Christmas spirit!

(looks back to window as she crosses to **BOB***'s table)*

Look at the snow, Lou! It's gonna be a white Christmas for sure! I just love a white Christmas!

(picks up coffee cup and heads for the coffee urn in the corner)

LOU. The weather or the song?

DARLENE. Both!

LOU. Is there anything about Christmas you don't love, Darlene?

DARLENE. Nothing I can think of, Lou!

BARBIE JO. *(on phone, agitated and exasperated with her mother)* No, Mom! Dave's not coming! I already told you that. Mom, please…what's done is done!

(pause)

What do you mean, "huffy"? I am not huf…

(pause)

"When something in life doesn't go my way?" That's not fair!

LOU. Darlene, it's been snowing on and off for three days now. How white do you want it to be?

DARLENE. My Jimmy loves snow! So does your Bill!

LOU. Yes, well… "My Bill" will wade through anything. Snow, mud, flood waters, our marriage. "My Bill" hasn't grown up yet.

BARBIE JO. Mama, I'll call you later. No, Mama. Dave's with Lou's Bill and Darlene's Jimmy. They went hunting.

(pause)

Yes, killing things on Christmas Eve.

(pause)

I know you would, Momma. If it weren't for the kids, I'd do it myself.

DARLENE. If you ask me, growing up is way overrated.

LOU. *(ignores* **DARLENE***'s comment)* Even Bill's work isn't grown up. Takin' folks hikin' up into the mountains. Why, he's more a big boy scout than a grown man.

DARLENE. Still, he's good to have around! Useful, you know?

LOU. Usually! That's why I can't figure out why he'd go huntin' today! It's not like him to go along with a scheme to get out of town on a holiday! Even if Dave was madder than a wet hen!

(sniffs)

Smoke!

(yells)

I smell smoke!

BARBIE JO. *(still on phone)* Smoke! Mama, I gotta go! My pies are burning!

LOU. *(smoke billows from the kitchen)* On fire's more like it! Darlene, get the fire extinguisher! Bob, you sit tight. We're gonna be a little longer with your pie!

*(***BARBIE JO*** *runs into the kitchen.* ***DARLENE*** *runs through kitchen door.* ***LOU*** *throws open the front door and fans the smoke with a menu as the bell above the door clangs loudly.)*

MARK. *(fans the smoke with his notebook)* Can I help, Miss Lou?

LOU. Never you mind, Mark. It's not the first time we've had to deal with second-hand smoke in here!

(still fanning smoke)

You could introduce yourself to Bob over there. His truck quit on him. Travis is workin' on it now.

MARK. *(waves to* **BOB***'s as he fans around his face)* Hi Bob… I'm Mark. Mark Riley.

BOB/NARRATOR. *(coughs and catches his breath)* Howdy, Mark! Right nice t'meet ya. I noticed you with a pile of books over there.

MARK. I was studying, but I can't see a thing now.

LOU. *(still fanning smoke out the front door)* Mark's in his first year of med school. His pop's our town doctor. We're hopin' Mark'll open up practice right here in Christmas when he graduates.

MARK. That's the plan, Miss Lou.

(picks up his books)

But in the meantime, I best be getting' home before that snow gets any deeper. And this smoke gets any thicker!

(takes his coat off the coat rack)

Nice to meet you, Bob.

(heads quickly for the door)

BOB/NARRATOR. Good luck with your studies, son. The world can always use another good doctor.

LOU. *(shouts out the door after the fleeing* **MARK***)* Merry Christmas, Mark!

MARK. *(offstage)* Merry Christmas, Miss Lou!

LOU. *(Closes the door. Cow bell clangs.)* Now there goes a nice boy. His father's a tough old bird. Has that boy studying night and day. Still, they come from a nice family. Riley senior's father was town doctor before I was born. My grandma said they used to pay him in milk and eggs.

BOB/NARRATOR. Seems I remember hearing stories like that from my grandma only it was bread and apples!

LOU. Times were simpler then, weren't they?

(yells toward kitchen)

How bad is it, Barbie Jo? Should I call the boys at the fire department?

*(***BARBIE JO*** *comes rushing in from the kitchen with soot on her cheek, carrying a very large, very burnt, very black pie.)*

BARBIE JO. No, but I'm gonna have to start all over again on these pies for the Salvation Army. I'll never make it to Della's in time to get my hair done!

(puts pie down on the center table)

BARBIE JO. *(cont.)* And look at my nails. My mother's plannin' on us bein' there by five. She gets ornerier than a cornered she-bear when we're late!

LOU. Now calm down, Barbie Jo! You're borrowing trouble when it's not needed. You look just fine!

BARBIE JO. *(straightens her apron)* I...aaah, I look like an unmade bed! That's another thing Mama hates – unmade beds!

LOU. Stop worrying about your mother! Just because *she* can't go a day without a buff and a polish, doesn't mean you have to.

THE KIWI SONG – **LOU & BARBIE JO**

LOU. Have I told you my theory about kiwis?

BARBIE JO. Nah, I think I missed that one, Lou.

LOU. Have a seat, Barbie Jo. You need to hear this.

BARBIE JO. Is this gonna take long?

LOU.

A KIWI IS QUITE SCARY;
IT'S LITTLE, BROWN, AND HAIRY.
NO ONE EVER THOUGHT
TO CHECK IT TWICE.

BUT SOMEONE IN OUR HISTORY;
SOLVED THE KIWI MYSTERY;
AND IF YOU'RE WISE
YOU'LL FOLLOW MY ADVICE.

BE A KIWI.
WHAT YOU LOOK LIKE MATTERS LESS
THAN WHAT IS ON THE INSIDE
WHEN YOU'RE FEELING LIKE A MESS.

BE A KIWI.
TELL 'EM FAR AND NEAR;
I'M A KIWI!
SHOUT IT LOUD AND CLEAR!

LOU. *(cont.)*

THE KIWI LOOKS QUITE FUNNY.
IT GROWS WHERE IT IS SUNNY.
YOU'LL NEVER FIND IT IN THE SNOW AND ICE.

OUT IN THAT HUMIDITY,
THEY OVERCAME STUPIDITY,
AND JUST ONE BITE
WAS ABLE TO SUFFICE.

BE A KIWI.
WHEN APPEARANCES YOU DOUBT,
PUT ASIDE THE OUTSIDE
AND LET THE INSIDE OUT.

BE A KIWI.
TELL 'EM FAR AND NEAR;
I'M A KIWI!
SHOUT IT LOUD AND CLEAR!

WHEN YOU LOOK AT WHAT'S INSIDE;
IF IT'S KIWI, IF IT'S YOU;
YOU'LL KNOW WHAT'S ON THE OUTSIDE,
ISN'T ALWAYS TRUE!

BE A KIWI.

BARBIE JO.

I'M A KIWI!
WHAT I LOOK LIKE MATTERS LESS
THAN WHAT IS ON THE INSIDE
WHEN I'M FEELING LIKE A MESS.

I'M A KIWI!
NO MATTER WHAT MOM DOES
I'M A KIWI!
AND I'M GREAT DESPITE THE FUZZ!

BOTH.

I'M A KIWI!
TELL 'EM FAR AND NEAR!
I'M A KIWI!
SHOUT IT LOUD AND SHOUT IT LOUD AND CLEAR!

LOU. Forget about Della's today, Barbie Jo. If your mother makes some sassy comment about your hair, tell her you baked pies for charity, and you felt that was more important than female vanity.

(pause)

If that doesn't shut her up, keep telling yourself, "I'm a kiwi."

BARBIE JO. Well, since nothing shuts Mama up, here goes…

(crosses to window, mutters)

I'm a kiwi. I'm a kiwi.

*(**DARLENE** rushes back into the room with a rather ominous looking fire extinguisher)*

DARLENE. *(to **LOU**)* Here's the fire extinguisher! You take it, Lou! I don't know what to do!

LOU. *(takes extinguisher)* Too late, Darlene.

(indicates burnt pie on table)

Atlanta's already burned to the ground.

DARLENE. *(notices the pie)* It looks delicious! Just the way I like it. Apple or cherry?

BARBIE JO. *(to **DARLENE**, harsh)* APPLE!

(mutters to herself)

I'm a kiwi… I'm a kiwi…

DARLENE. That's my favorite. Burnt apple. My Jimmy likes it too. Least ways, he says he does! Of course, I usually spray it with a pile of whipped cream and throw some fresh cinnamon on top.

BARBIE JO. *(light bulb comes on)* Darlene, you might be right! If I cover these pies with a thick layer of whipped cream, nobody'll know the difference!

*(**BARBIE JO** runs behind the counter for the whipped cream.)*

LOU. Barbie Jo, do you really want to donate burnt pies to the Salvation Army to feed the homeless on Christmas Day?

BARBIE JO. Why not?

(shakes can vigorously and sprays the pie with a huge pile of whipped cream)

There! Go ahead, Darlene – tell me how it tastes.

DARLENE. Can I have a little more whipped cream?

LOU. *(scoops up the pie)* No, no, now stop this. There's no way I'm letting' Darlene eat this!

DARLENE. Why not, Lou?

LOU. 'Cause that black stuff on the top usually means, "Not fit for human consumption"!

(exasperated)

Darlene – don't you have customers to take care of?

DARLENE. *(looks around)* Um, not really. No one left except Bob…

LOU. Then find something useful to do with yourself! Geesh!

DARLENE. Bob, would you like to sing some Christmas carols while you're waitin' on your truck?

BOB/NARRATOR. I like Christmas music and all, Darlene, but I'm not much of a singer.

BARBIE JO. *(at the window again)* Darlene, leave that poor man alone! He doesn't need to listen to you singing "Jingle Bells." That's more suffering than any visitor should have to endure! Give him some peace!

(mutters)

I'm a kiwi… I'm a kiwi…

LOU. *(goes behind counter and tosses pie away)* You're both drivin' me crazy, is what you're doin'! I'm startin' to itch! It's Christmas Eve, and I'm itchin'and twitchin'! Stop arguing, and get back to work!

*(**DARLENE** has started singing "Jingle Bells" badly. This is quiet in the background. Noticeable, but does not overpower dialogue.)*

Now don't be lookin' out that window again, Barbie Jo!

BARBIE JO. But look at the snow!

LOU. You know your Dave and that mangy crew'll be just fine. They'll be home with their tails between their legs before your Mama gets Christmas dinner on the table.

(yells at **DARLENE***)*

Darlene! Stop that caterwauling. It sounds like you're field dressing a cat over there.

DARLENE. Sorry, Lou. You know me. I get a carried away!

BARBIE JO. I'm a kiwi. I'm a kiwi.

LOU. *(to* **BARBIE JO***)* Stop muttering, "I'm a kiwi." Save it for later – when you really need it!

BARBIE JO. I can't help it! My Dave's the best butcher in the county! Every year he brings a prize turkey to Mama's for Christmas Eve dinner. Not this year – this year he decides to go huntin' for supper. If I know him, he'll probably bring home a skunk!

DARLENE. Just to be a stinker!

(laughs at her own joke)

BARBIE JO. *(sobs)* Besides pickin' at me about my hair and nails, Mama's gonna have a field day with this!

LOU. Dave wouldn't do that to you. He's a fine husband, and a good father. He knows what your mama's like. Dave may be in a snit, but he won't make things worse than they already are!

BARBIE JO. He's still a guy! It's Christmas Eve. Instead playing in the snow with his buddies, Dave should be home with Robby and Becky readin' "Twas the Night Before Christmas" and singin' "Hark the Herald Angels Sing."

DARLENE. Oh, I love that one...

(sings wrong lyrics:)

HARK, HAROLD THE ANGEL SINGS,
GLORY TO THE NEWBORN KING.

LOU. Not now, Darlene.

BARBIE JO. *(ignores* **DARLENE***)* Rolling around on the floor. Rough housing like they do. Spilling their hot cocoa and puking up Christmas cookies. It's tradition!

LOU. You worry too much, Barbie Jo. Now stop it.

BARBIE JO. That's easy for you to say. You and Bill don't have kids.

LOU. Well, we're tryin'! Course, Bill will be spared the joy of having kids climbing on him and puking up Christmas cookies this year.

DARLENE. Do all kids puke?

BARBIE JO. Sooner or later, Darlene. Why?

DARLENE. Just thinkin' Jimmy won't be too happy if our kids puke. He can't even look at spoiled milk without turning green! He has a very delicate system!

BARBIE JO. So you think you're gonna marry Jimmy and have kids?

DARLENE. I might. I just need to change a few things.

BARBIE JO. What kind of things?

DARLENE. Just a few Jimmy things. I figure once we're married, I can change him. Ain't that how it works, Lou?

LOU. Yeah, they all change after they're married.

BARBIE JO. Ain't that the truth!

(hesitantly)

Did I tell you Dave cleaned up that old cabin out back of the house? He put in insulation and ran cable to a TV box out there. I think he plans to use it as a hideout. He doesn't love me anymore! He doesn't love our kids. My marriage is over!

DARLENE. *(reaches to comfort* **BARBIE JO***)* Oh nooooo…

LOU. All right! I want both you girls to calm down. Barbie Jo, you know Dave loves you. He loves Robby and Becky. He even puts up with your mama. Maybe he just needs a little space right now. Guys are like that sometimes.

(looks out the window)

Good Lord, that snow's really comin' down!

*(Everyone looks out the window at the falling snow. All but **DARLENE** look worried. Characters in the diner freeze. **BOB/NARRATOR** addresses audience.)*

BOB/**NARRATOR.** Now Barbie Jo's Dave and Lou's Bill and Darlene's Jimmy went into them mountains today to go huntin'. Dave's avoidin' Christmas Eve with his mother-in-law, Verna Belle. He didn't mind the fact that the 'all guy' huntin' trip also got him away from his sweet little kids. Seems Dave has had his fill of being a family man, at least for the moment.

(pause)

Dave's usin' this huntin' trip to make a point. He's forcin' Barbie Jo to decide where her loyalties lie. It's Christmas Eve with him and the kids at home, or off to suffer through another miserable Christmas Eve dinner with her mother.

(pause)

Barbie Jo's making a point too. She believes traditions, no matter how distasteful, must be honored and upheld. Seems to me a lot of poor choices are being made just to make a point. Usually, it just stirs the pot.

(pause)

Now those boys up in them mountains had a big part to play in the story that was unfolding. The storm and all this snow just made sure they were where they had to be, when they had to be there.

(Lights cross-fade to Scene Two.)

Scene Two

(Inside of a rough mountain cabin. Front door is upstage with a moose head hanging over it. A window on one side of the door shows heavy snow falling. Cabin is furnished with an old sofa and coffee table and a chair and hassock off to one side. There is a bar with two bar stools to the right of the door, in front of the window upstage left. Another doorway leads to a hallway and bath upstage left. An old wood stove sits stage left of the couch. We see **DAVE**, **BILL**, *and* **JIMMY** *enter, covered in snow. Each one is wearing an outlandish hunting hat, which will come into play later. Hats should be big and crazy – each one unique in its design.)*

DAVE. I swear Jimmy, I don't think you could catch a cold much less a deer!

BILL. Could you make any more noise out there?!

DAVE. Whooo, between the stink and the noise, we're never gonna bag a buck!

(fanning his nose)

Why don't you just hang a flashing sign that says "Deer Hunters hiding here!"

JIMMY. Hey, that tweren't my fault. I didn't know we were comin' up here when I made that monster batch of chili. I usually stick to SPAM when I know we're goin' hunting. I have a very delicate stomach.

BILL. Delicate!

(shaking his head)

After you eat chili, your body should be registered with the Department of Defense as a weapon of mass destruction.

DAVE. Talk about standing upwind! By the time you were done, there was a two foot snowdrift behind you!

BILL. I guess this means you boys are ready to head back to town, eh?

DAVE. No, why? You giving up already…

   (glares at **JIMMY.** *)*

   …just because of one little setback?

BILL. No. Just makin' sure you hadn't changed your mind.

DAVE. Change my mind? It was you asked Otis if we could use his cabin.

BILL. Yeah, but it was you who said you wanted to get away from Barbie Jo, and Jimmy said he wanted to get away from Darlene.

JIMMY. That's because you said you wanted to get away from Lou Lou!

BILL. *(to* **DAVE***)* Look, all's I'm saying is since our sophomore year, I can't remember a Christmas Eve when you and Barbie Jo weren't together. It's just not like you to be away on Christmas Eve because of a little unpleasantness from Verna Belle. You oughta be used to it by now!

DAVE. I had to show Barbie Jo who wears the pants in this family.

JIMMY. *(sarcastically)* And just who would that be?

DAVE. Every year Barbie Jo drags me off to her mother's for Christmas Eve dinner. Then, midnight service at the church.

BILL. I wonder what Lou's makin' for dinner this year. That woman sure can cook!

DAVE. *(ignores* **BILL***)* In between, her mother spends the entire night nagging and advising! Tellin' me how to run my business, how to cut my hair, what I should eat, like I need help with that!

JIMMY. You are a fine eater, Dave!

DAVE. And then…then, after dessert, she starts in on how Barbie Jo should have married that jerk Lance Madison over at the real estate office 'stead of me!

BILL. So, have a few cold ones, and tune her out! That's what I do!

DAVE. I tried that, and it used to work, but the kids are getting older, and they've started to understand! I had to put my foot down or give up my dignity completely.

JIMMY. Yeah, well you done such a good job puttin' your foot down that you really stepped in it this time! You're up here with us while Barbie Jo and the kids are eatin' ham at Grandma's. Verna Belle finally won!

DAVE. What do you mean she won?

JIMMY. She got rid of you for Christmas! That's what she's wanted all along!

BILL. Now you guys are bein' a bit rough on Dave's Monster-In-Law, don't ya think? My Lou Lou says Verna Belle ain't so bad. She's kinda like a kiwi!

JIMMY. Kiwi? What's that?

DAVE. Beats the hell out of me. Can't be anything good.

BILL. Lou says Verna Belle doesn't really hate you, Dave. She just wishes your profession was something classier than butcherin' hogs! Lou says all the meat and blood gets to her.

DAVE. Lou said all that?

BILL. Yep. That and a lot more.

DAVE. Well forget about what Lou says. I wanna know what you say.

BILL. I got nothin' to say other than what Lou says.

DAVE. She says it's about time you and her had a family. Is that what you say? Are you ready to adopt somebody else's kid? No! That's why you're up here hidin' from Lou Lou and smellin' Jimmy's recycled chili, ain't it?

BILL. Well, I...

DAVE. Let's face it! We're all up here to get away from the women!

JIMMY. *(thoughtfully)* Can't live with 'em. Can't...can't...

BILL. Well, genius? Can't what?

JIMMY. Can't nothing!

DAVE. Only you ain't livin' with Darlene! You're just paying her a friendly visit every now and then. Ain't that right, Jimbo?

BILL. Yeah, well, everything has its limits. Right, Jimmy? Time constraints?

JIMMY. Time outs, ya mean. Like when my pa made me stand in the corner.

DAVE. With the pointed hat on.

JIMMY. That was a double billed cap!

DAVE. A dunce cap is what it was!

BILL. Hey, hey, hey! Let's all calm down.

(**JIMMY** *and* **DAVE** *glare at each other.*)

Have another one.

(**BILL** *and* **JIMMY** *reach for another cold can.*)

DAVE. All I'm sayin' is there comes a time when a man's gotta do what a man's gotta do! It was time for me to stand up for myself. I was hoping Barbie Jo'd agree to stay home this year, but she insisted we go to her mother's. "It's tradition," she says. Well, I'm starting a new tradition, and it's got nothin' to do Verna Belle Jenkins!

JIMMY. What's the new tradition? Christmas presents made from fishing lures?

DAVE. No, you knucklehead! This is! The new tradition is we come up here for some guy time and hunting on Christmas Eve! Bill, you can teach Jimmy and me some of those survival skills you learned in the army. We'll be like Rambo with mistletoe!

JIMMY. How festive!

DAVE. Barbie Jo has to decide between me and that alligator she calls mama!

BILL. Alligator?

DAVE. *(goes to cooler, pops open can)* Yep, gators're one of the few species known to eat their young! I need a cold one.

BILL. Well, this feud between you and Verna Belle doesn't sound very Christmassy for Barbie Jo! Did you ever think of that?

DAVE. Not really.

BILL. Listen, if we're starting a new tradition, promise me you'll keep Jimmy away from the chili next year!

DAVE. I'm for that!

BILL. As a matter of fact, I'll bring some of Lou's bran muffins – just in case.

(lifts can in air)

Well, here's to guys still bein' guys!

(They all down the contents of their cans. Afterwards, DAVE crushes his can against his forehead. JIMMY belches.)

It's comin' out both ends now!

DAVE. One good swallow deserves another.

(He hand out three more cans.)

BILL. If you guys are determined to stay up here, let's grab some grub and head back out. If Jimmy's done with his silly symphony, we could still bring home some fresh venison for Christmas dinner!

JIMMY. My delicate system seems to have quieted some.

DAVE. Yeah, well if your 'delicate system' acts up again, I have some duct tape in the truck!

BILL. Speaking of the truck…Jimmy, why don't you head out there and get a couple packages of Slim Jims and some pork rinds. Oh, and check the weather report.

(pause)

That snow was coming down hard and heavy when we came in. Lou won't appreciate me getting' stuck up here with you guys overnight.

DAVE. Might be a nice quiet way to spend Christmas. Snowed in with just the guys!

BILL. Otis said there isn't much firewood up here. He isn't plannin' to use the cabin much this winter, so there's no provisions. All we have is the pork rinds and the beer nuts.

JIMMY. And the beer!

BILL. And the beer. Let's just keep an eye on the weather, Okay?

JIMMY. *(Putting his hunting gear back on. Makes a big deal of adjusting his hats – first a stocking cap which looks ridiculous and then a big silly hunting hat.)* Listen, I like you fellas and all, but I can't get snowed in up here either. I expect to be unwrapping my Christmas present tonight, and it's a darn site prettier than either of you!

DAVE. Oh? You payin' Darlene a visit?

JIMMY. Well, nothing official or anything, but we do have a standing date for Christmas Eve. I'm sure she's expecting me to light her Yule Log!

BILL. Well, just keep your lighter in your pocket 'til you're sure Darlene's there alone, Romeo! Lou Lou mentioned Keith Parker from the Rotary Club's been sniffing around the diner asking questions 'bout you and Darlene. From what Lou says, Darlene hasn't completely shut him down!

DAVE. Keith Parker? Ain't he the guy with the highlights in his hair and the plucked eyebrows?

BILL. Yep. Hear he bikini waxes his chest hairs, too.

JIMMY. What? Well, Darlene isn't interested in anybody prettier than she is!

DAVE. Good for you!

JIMMY. Nope! Darlene only has eyes for her Jimmy Boy!

DAVE. Eyes can wander, Jimmy Boy!

JIMMY. Our personal ads on the internet said we were a perfect match! She wouldn't break a standing date.

(pause)

Even if I forgot to mention it to her.

(concerned)

Would she?

DAVE. Shrimp happens, Jimbo! Like that time you got expelled for putting gum on Mrs. Maxwell's chair.

JIMMY. Gee, that was fun! Three days out of school. How is that punishment?

BILL. Pay attention, Jimbo. Women can be funny about an arrangement like yours and Darlene's. Especially when you aren't married yet. They get going on and on about being taken for granted, and before you know it, you're sleeping with the dog on the couch!

JIMMY. Dog! I don't like dogs! I'm more of a cat person! Cats think like us, ya know? Smart, cunning, sleek…

BILL. Women don't think like us, pal. Cats maybe, but women? Never!

DAVE. Cats? I thought guys were supposed to have minds like loyal old dogs!

JIMMY. My ma always said us boys were more like hogs than dogs!

BILL. Guys are like a lot of animals. I'm tryin' to explain to you about women!

DAVE. Go right ahead. Enlighten us.

BILL. Being hitched to a woman is a lot like bein' a bee keeper. Most of the time, the bees are busy doin' whatever it is they do, and everybody's happy. Why, the bee keeper don't mind the investment and daily care 'cause every once in a while, he gets a little honey out of the hive.

BEEHIVE – BILL, DAVE, & JIMMY

BILL.

GOT ME A BEEHIVE AND MY LOU LOU IS THE QUEEN.
SHE RUNS THE SHOW, BUT DON'T YOU KNOW,
SHE'S NEVER REALLY MEAN.
SHE SAYS I CAN'T BE TRUSTED TO KEEP MYSELF IN LINE.
GOT ME A BEEHIVE, BUT THINGS WILL BE JUST FINE.

DAVE & JIM.

BUZZA BUZZA, BUZZA BUZZ BUZZ.
BUZZA BUZZA, BUZZA BUZZ BUZZ.

BILL.

> I'M LUCKY TO BE MARRIED TO THE BEST OF ALL QUEEN BEES.
> SHE KEEPS THE HONEY FLOWIN', I'M HAPPY AS CAN BE.
> SEEMS JUST ONCE IN A WHILE SHE'D TRUST ME TO BE WISE.
> AND LET ME DO SOME HUNTIN' – SPEND TIME WITH JUST
>   THE GUYS.
>
> GOT ME A BEEHIVE AND MY LOU LOU IS THE QUEEN.
> SHE RUNS THE SHOW, BUT DON'T YOU KNOW,
> SHE'S NEVER REALLY MEAN
> I LISTEN TO HER NAGGIN', I HARDLY EVER WHINE.
> GOT ME A BEEHIVE, BUT THINGS WILL BE JUST FINE.

DAVE & JIM.

> BUZZA BUZZA, BUZZA BUZZ BUZZ.
> BUZZA BUZZA, BUZZA BUZZ BUZZ.

BILL.

> MY QUEEN BEE LOVES HER HONEY, SHE KEEPS ME WARM AT
>   NIGHT.
> I DO THE WORK, PAY ALL THE BILLS, WE ALMOST NEVER
>   FIGHT.
> I KEEP MY EYES RIGHT ON THE PRIZE, DON'T BUZZ NO
>   OTHER BEES.
> SHE LETS ME KISS HER ROYAL HAND WHEN I GET DOWN ON
>   MY KNEES.
>
> GOT ME A BEEHIVE AND MY LOU LOU IS THE QUEEN.
> SHE RUNS THE SHOW, BUT DON'T YOU KNOW,
> SHE'S NEVER REALLY MEAN.
> SHE THINKS SHE'S BOSS OF EVERYTHING, NOTHIN'S REALLY
>   MINE.
> GOT ME A BEEHIVE, BUT THINGS WILL BE JUST FINE

DAVE & JIM.

> BUZZA BUZZA, BUZZA BUZZ BUZZZZZZZZZZ

JIMMY. So this is a 'birds & bees' story, right?

DAVE. No, you idiot! All Bill's sayin' is women fancy themselves the Queen Bee! They expect the best of everything and don't tolerate no rivals.

BILL. That's right. A pretty little honey bee walks by in a mini skirt and smiles at you friendly like, and the queen'll get her for sure!

DAVE. Ain't that the truth!

BILL. The queen decides when she mates, too. I think I read somewhere she kills the poor male once they've finished their business.

DAVE. No, that's the grasshoper. She eats his head off when they're done!

BILL. No, that's the praying mantis.

JIMMY. Sure are a lot of mean spirited bugs, ain't there!

BILL. If you're dealin' with just one bee, you're fairly safe, but if you're surrounded by the entire hive, you better have your bee keepin' mask pulled down tight. Ya got me?

JIMMY. My head hurts.

(walks to cooler, grabs a can)

I need another one.

DAVE. *(swipes beer from* **JIMMY***)* Wait. Give me that! You're supposed to check the weather, remember?

JIMMY. Save some for me. My finely honed huntin' skills are sharpest after I've had my first six pack!

(Gust of snow hits him in face as he opens door.)

I hate snow! Whoever it was sang about "White Christmas" ought to be shot!

*(***JIMMY*** exits.)*

BILL. *(crossing to bar)* I need a fresh one. How 'bout you?

DAVE. You bet!

(sits on bar stool)

Besides, if I drink these fast, I'll be able to write my whole name in the snow!

BILL. *(behind bar)* I don't mind telling ya I'm glad to get away from Lou's talk about that adoption stuff for a few hours. Lord knows that woman wants a baby, but yapping at me every minute of the day doesn't help.

DAVE. Count your lucky stars! Do you know how tired I am of being climbed on, rolled on, pounded on, puked on every second of the day! Those kids think I'm their own personal jungle gym! I have more bruises than a week old banana!

BILL. Really?

DAVE. Would I lie to you? I can't wait to start usin' my hideout cabin for some peace and quiet. I finished installing the last of the insulation over Thanksgiving. That old place don't look like much, but it's gonna be great!

BILL. Barbie Jo don't mind?

DAVE. I love Barbie Jo, but with Verna Belle and the young'ns around, I need a place to get away. Trust me. Lou Lou may want to be a mother, but fatherhood ain't all it's cracked up to be!

BILL. It can't be that bad. Can it?

(pause)

No, don't answer that!

DAVE. Remember the summer you raised that calf for 4-H?

BILL. Yeah.

DAVE. It's like that, but without the blue ribbon at the end.

BILL. Geeze. Still…Lou Lou's set on being a mother, so I don't see as I have much choice. I never knew adoption was so tough though.

DAVE. Bad, huh?

BILL. The worst! I think I'd make a good dad, but I'm not as young as I used to be. I hate to think my best fatherin' years are behind me.

DAVE. You do need energy to keep up with them.

BILL. Maybe we could get one of those baby leashes for when I need a break! Or a kennel!

DAVE. Worked when I was trainin' my hound!

BILL. If it's real bad, I can always come hang out with you at the hideout! Got room for one more?

DAVE. Sure, the welcome mat's always out for a fellow weary father.

(pause)

You do what you want with the adoption and all, but when it comes to kids, Jimmy's probably the smartest guy I know.

BILL. *(incredulous)* Jimmy's the smartest?! Why's that?

DAVE. 'Cause he's been smart enough never to get married in the first place!

(They hold up their cans and toast each other.)

BOTH. Cheers!

Scene Three

*(Back inside Lou's Diner. Snow is falling as **BOB/ NARRATOR** looks out the window. He appears to be concerned about the weather. **LOU** is in the kitchen with **BARBIE JO**, who is on the phone. **DARLENE** reads the side of the fire extinguisher trying to figure out how to use it. She stops to pump the top, then sticks the end of a fork into the nozzle and looks directly into it. **BOB** watches.)*

BOB. Darlene, honey. I don't like to pry, but do you know what you're doin' with that fire extinguisher?

DARLENE. Not really. But these instructions seem pretty simple.

BOB. Lou! I think you might want to come out here. Darlene's fixin' to use the fire extinguisher!

LOU. *(entering from kitchen)* Darlene, what're you up to?

DARLENE. I was thinkin' we could spray some fire extinguisher foam on the window! Make it look like snow! I see it all the time on the windows in the big city department stores.

LOU. Darlene, put that fire extinguisher away! Girl, it's snowin' between your ears!

*(**DARLENE** crosses to the counter with the fire extinguisher as **BARBIE JO** comes bounding out of the kitchen talking to her mother on the cell phone.)*

BARBIE JO. Wait a minute, Mom. I'm bakin' pies for the Salvation Army. That's more important than female vanity, isn't it?

(to herself)

I'm a kiwi. I'm a kiwi.

(back to phone)

Because I love him, Mama!

(pause)

BARBIE JO. *(cont.)* No. No one says you have to love him too. Just be nice! If not for my sake and the kids' then for the sake of the season!

(pause)

I know you wish I wouldn't have married him! But then you wouldn't have your grandchildren!

(pause)

Sperm bank! That's it! The bell just rang on my pies! Goodbye, Mama!

(hangs up and drops exhausted into a chair)

I'm a kiwi. I'm a kiwi.

LOU. Well?

BARBIE JO. Well what? Momma's as mad as a treed possum, that new batch of pies isn't cookin' fast enough, and I look like an unmade bed!

DARLENE. *(She crosses out from behind the counter, where she absent-mindedly leaves the fire extinguisher.)* An unmade bed? You already used that one, Barbie Jo.

BARBIE JO. *(ignores* **DARLENE,** *keeps talking to* **LOU***)* And it's all because of Dave! Why, Lou? Why would he do this to me? I'd never leave *him* on Christmas Eve to go hunting!

LOU. Well, now Barbie Jo – men area different than us. Take Dave. Well, he's basically like a cat!

DARLENE. I love cats! There must be half dozen out at the barn. They follow me all over!

BARBIE JO. Must be males!

DARLENE. Come to think of it, they are!

LOU. There! See what I mean, Barbie Jo! Men are like cats! You scratch a cat in the right place, keep it fed and warm, and it's happy as can be. Just don't expect it to come when you call!

BARBIE JO. Why not?

LOU. It's like this, Barbie Jo...

CATTIN' AROUND – LOU, BARBIE JO & DARLENE

LOU.

WE DO OUR BEST TO KEEP HOME NICE.
OPEN THE DOOR HE DON'T THINK TWICE.
HE'S OUT WITH HIS FRIENDS, OUT ON THE TOWN.
CAN'T KEEP A MAN FROM CATTIN' AROUND.

HE'S PETTED AND STROKED, HE LOVES HIS BED.
NO OTHER PET IS SO WELL FED.
HE HAS SOME GOOD POINTS, BUT I HAVE FOUND.
IT WON'T BE LONG 'TIL HE'S CATTIN' AROUND.

LOU.

ONLY AS LOYAL AS HE WANTS TO BE.

GIRLS.

MEOW OW OW

LOU.

TURNS UP HIS NOSE WHEN I CALL.

GIRLS.

MEOW OW OW

LOU.

SO FAR HE'S ALWAYS COME HOME TO ME.

GIRLS.

MEOW OW OW

LOU.

IF HE COMES HOME AT ALL.

LOU.

ONLY AS LOYAL AS HE WANTS TO BE.

GIRLS.

MEOW OW OW

LOU.

TURNS UP HIS NOSE WHEN I CALL.

GIRLS.

MEOW OW OW

LOU.

SO FAR HE'S ALWAYS COME HOME TO ME.

GIRLS.

MEOW OW OW

LOU.

IF HE COMES HOME AT ALL.

LOU.

SO IF YOU WANT A PET THAT'S LOYAL AND TRUE.

GIRLS.

MEOW

LOU.

ONE THAT'S ALWAYS THERE WITH YOU.

GIRLS.

MEOW

LOU.

INVEST IN A DOG, A TRUSTY OL' HOUND.

CAN'T KEEP A MAN FROM CATTIN' AROUND.

OH, HE'S CATTIN' AROUND.

HE'S CATTIN' AROUND.

CATTIN' AROUND.

BARBIE JO. You're not saying Bill is…Bill is…

LOU. Bill is what?

BARBIE JO. A philanderer!

LOU. He's independent, Barbie Jo! Not suicidal!

BARBIE JO. He tryin' to prove he's still independent?

LOU. Right! Like this stunt today!

DARLENE. I still think Jimmy's more of a dog person!

BARBIE JO. Hard to say what animal Jimmy is, Darlene!

LOU. Like cats, men mess up the furniture and leave hair in places you wish you hadn't looked. Thank God they're cute and playful once in a while, or what woman in her right mind would have one?!

DARLENE. I once read they sleep ninety percent of every day! Ain't that somethin'?

BARBIE JO. Ninety percent?!

DARLENE. Cats! Not men!

BARBIE JO. So what you're saying is there's no hope at all, and I should take Dave to the vet and have him put to sleep?

LOU. There's always hope, Barbie Jo. I'm just sayin' don't expect a man to roll over and beg! Expect him to act more like a cat than a dog, and you won't be disappointed when he takes off like today!

BARBIE JO. I hope he gets fleas!

DARLENE. And ticks!

(**BARBIE JO** *glares in annoyance.*)

Just tryin' to help!

LOU. Cats are smart enough to know when they've got it good. They usually find their way home.

DARLENE. *(indignant)* Well, so do dogs! That's why I want my Jimmy to get me a dog for Christmas. Wouldn't that be terrific, Lou!

LOU. And who's gonna take care of a dog when you're here ten hours a day? You've already got three horses, two goats, and a barn load of chickens!

DARLENE. If my Jimmy bought me a dog, he'd help take care of it.

BARBIE JO. Are you serious? Jimmy can't even take care of himself!

DARLENE. Well, I know that…but that's one of the things I'll change after we're married.

BARBIE JO. Change Jimmy?! Ha! Darlene, what are you thinkin'? You signed up on that dating website, ah… what was it called, Lou?

LOU. Clod Hoppers.com

BARBIE JO. That's right. Clodhoppers.com! And what was their slogan?

LOU. "We cater to bulls and beauties…"

BARBIE JO. What kind of man'd you expect to meet on a website like that? You're lucky he's not Larry the Cable Guy!

DARLENE. Well, I tried datin' city boys, but they don't understand me!

BARBIE JO. Darlene, nobody understands you!

DARLENE. One fella wanted me to live in the city. He said I could stable my horses in his garage! Can you imagine! I can't see a guy like that muckin' out my stalls, no sirree!

BARBIE JO. But Jimmy's a hog farmer! One of the boys here in town might suit you better. Keith Parker for instance.

DARLENE. Keith Parker! Do you know he highlights his hair and plucks his eyebrows? Della says he spends more time in her salon than I do! No, I'm gonna marry my Jimmy! He just doesn't know it yet!

(The front door is suddenly thrown open. **MARK RILEY** *enters amid the clambering of the cow bell, a large burst of snow, and the howling of the wind. He is bundled up warmly in his coat which is now covered with snow.)*

MARK. *(Grabs the door to keep from falling as he tries to close it against the wind.)* That front step's gettin' a might slippery, Miss Lou!

LOU. Mark, what're you doin' here? I thought you'd be halfway home by now!

MARK. *(Finally manages to close door, he's in a hurry.)* I forgot Ma's pie. She'll skin me alive if I don't bring it for Christmas dinner!

LOU. We're havin' some trouble today with the pies, Mark.

MARK. Ma won't be happy! Do you have one in back? Something saved up for a rainy day? Anything, Miss Lou. Please!

(stamps his feet and dusts snow off his coat)

LOU. Let's see what I can find.

MARK. I ran into Travis in town, Bob. He said your truck'd be ready in less than an hour! Looks like you'll make it home tonight after all!

BOB. That's great news! Thanks, Mark! I'm enjoyin' the company, but it'd be right nice to get back to the interstate before this snow gets much deeper.

MARK. That reminds me, Miss Lou... There's a stranger out front – just standin' in the snow.

LOU. What? Where?

MARK. Out front.

DARLENE. What kind of stranger?

BARBIE JO. How many kinds are there?

MARK. A girl. I ran into her outside. She said her name's Mary Sue and she just got off the bus, but she doesn't want to come inside. I think she needs help, Miss Lou.

BARBIE JO. Help? What're you talkin' about, Mark?

LOU. *(to **BARBIE JO**)* Now hold on here. Wait a minute.

*(to **MARK**)*

Are you sure? There's no bus comes through here Christmas Eve. Used to be one from Ridgewood, but that was a morning bus. And it stopped runnin' years ago.

MARK. Well, she's out there all right.

(moves to window)

Come see for yourself. She's just standin' there by the bus stop.

*(**LOU**, **BARBIE JO**, and **DARLENE** crowd around the window and peer out, each pulling the other aside to get a better look.)*

DARLENE. I don't see no one.

BARBIE JO. Neither do I, Darlene. Mark, you picked a bad day to pull a prank! I'm not in the mood! Wow! Look at that snow!

*(Unseen, **MARY SUE ARCHER** quietly enters from the kitchen.)*

MARK. It's not a prank, Barbie Jo! She's right there!

*(Points out window, but sees **MARY SUE** is gone. **MARK** is bewildered.)*

Well, golly! She was right there! I swear it!

BARBIE JO. Sure. And she just disappeared into the snow, like a Christmas angel, right?

MARK. Gosh, Barbie Jo, I don't know where she went, but she was there a minute ago.

(MARY SUE has entered quietly through kitchen door and put her duffel bag on the floor at the end of the counter. Her hair is wet and her coat doesn't quite close over her pregnant stomach. She wears a ratty scarf, and there are holes in her gloves. She looks tired and hungry, yet at the same time, she has an innocent glow about her.)

BOB. *(seeing girl)* Ah, Miss Lou. Looks like you've got company.

LOU. *(turns)* What's that, Bob?

BOB. *(nods toward MARY SUE)* It appears Mark's stranger has changed her mind.

LOU. *(seeing MARY SUE for first time – shocked)* Well, I'll be…

(MARK, BARBIE JO, and DARLENE turn around to find MARY SUE standing dripping wet at the end of the counter. All the characters freeze in tableau, representing their amazement.)

BOB. *(slowly, to the audience)* Now right off, somethin' about that girl caught my eye. It didn't hit me she was pregnant 'til Lou took her coat and set her down at the table next to mine. She looked sad and lost – the way an orphaned animal looks when it's tryin' to find its momma. She seemed young and fragile. That pregnant bump looked so out of place. I couldn't help but watch to see how this new chapter of my Christmas story was going to unfold.

LOU. *(genuinely shocked that someone entered her place without causing the bell to ring. Tableau is broken.)* How'd you get in here? I didn't hear the bell.

DARLENE. *(Reaches past LOU who is still in shock and extends her hand to MARY SUE.)* You must be Mary Sue! I'm Darlene! Nice t'meet ya!

LOU. *(comes to her senses)* Good grief! Where are my manners? Come in and sit down, honey. How...how'd you get in here? Oh, never mind that! I'm Lou, you've already met Mark here – and our Darlene. This is Barbie Jo, and that's Bob. He's just visitin'.

*(Takes **MARY SUE**'s coat as she leads her to a table. Looks at **BOB** and **BARBIE JO** to see their reaction to **MARY SUE**'s pregnancy.)*

Let me take that wet coat.

(Takes her coat and hangs it on the back of a chair.)

MARY SUE. Thank you, ma'am. I didn't realize how cold I was. It's sure nice and toasty in here!

BARBIE JO. *(exasperated)* Been bakin' pies all mornin', honey. Half the afternoon too! I'm burnin' up myself! I'll get you a slice in a minute if you've a mind to wait.

DARLENE. *(to **MARY SUE**)* Hope you like whipped cream!

MARY SUE. I do. But I can't stay long. I'll just get warmed up and be on my way.

LOU. On your way? But you still haven't told us where you came from... What bus you took... How'd you get here?

MARY SUE. *(confused)* I'm not really sure. Truth be told, I don't even know exactly why I got off the bus when I did. I heard the driver announce: *"Christmas! Next stop, Christmas,"* and I gazed out at the town.

(looks off into space, dreamily)

It looked so friendly. And safe. Like the world just stopped and everything grew quiet and still and peaceful and...well, here I am!

DARLENE. Welcome to Christmas!

MARY SUE. Sometimes it's like I hear this voice in my head. It usually points me in the right direction, so I've gotten used to doin' what it says.

BARBIE JO. *(sarcastically)* Great! *Just* great! Darlene, this a friend of yours?

DARLENE. *(goes to* **MARY SUE** *and comforts her)* Now there's nothin' wrong with listenin' to that voice in your head, Barbie Jo. My great grandma Maud used to say it was God's way of speakin' to your heart – tellin' you what He wants you to do.

MARY SUE. *(like* **DARLENE** *has just voiced something she's been thinking for months)* That's it exactly! That's how it seemed! Like God himself wanted me to stop here in Christmas.

BARBIE JO. *(watching the two girls bond)* Great! They're both one card short of a full deck!

LOU. *(scolding gently)* Barbie Jo, leave 'em alone. They ain't doin' no harm.

BARBIE JO. Fine. Drawer needs countin' anyway.

(goes behind counter and opens the drawer to count the cash)

*(*DARLENE *nods at* BARBIE JO *triumphantly as* LOU *continues speaking to* MARY SUE.)*

LOU. Well, no matter the reason, we're glad you're here, Mary Sue. Are you staying with family here in town?

MARY SUE. I don't have family. Except the baby, of course.

DARLENE. *(puts her hand on* **MARY SUE***'s stomach)* In here?

(excited – claps her hands)

That's amazin'! When's it due?

MARY SUE. Next week. I'm hopin' there'll be a hospital. If not, I'll manage somehow. I always do.

BARBIE JO. There's no hotels in town. If you're not stayin' with family, you'll have a tough time findin' a bed tonight.

MARY SUE. *(She gets up and starts putting on her coat.)* I usually go to the homeless shelter. I'll head that way after I dry off if you'll point me in the right direction.

DARLENE. Well now – hold on. We ain't got no homeless shelter here in Christmas either. I suppose it's 'cuz we ain't got no homeless.

BARBIE JO. That, and everybody in town's related to everybody else.

(*pause*)

We're bakin' pies for the Salvation Army to have at their shelter in Springfield tomorrow. But that's one county over.

MARK. Here, let me help with that, Mary Sue.

(*Helps* **MARY SUE** *put on her coat, then turns to* **LOU**.)

Maybe I should call my Dad – see if he can check her out.

MARY SUE. (*panicked*) What? No, please. I don't need to be checked!

LOU. Calm down, honey. Mark's daddy's our town doctor. When was the last time you had a check-up?

(**MARY SUE** *lowers her eyes guiltily.*)

Uh huh, I though so.

MARK. What do you think, Miss Lou?

LOU. It's not a bad idea, Mark. Your pa can check the baby, and we can call Sheriff Bradley to see about...

(*sniffs*)

SMOKE! I smell smoke!

BARBIE JO. (*runs into kitchen screaming*) Not again!

(*Large billows of smoke pour from the kitchen. Everyone goes into panic mode as unnoticed,* **MARY SUE** *leaves the restaurant. It would be a delight to see her disappear in one big cloud of smoke.*)

LOU. (*Extinguisher is not where it should be.*) Darlene, where's that fire extinguisher?

DARLENE. (*panicked*) It's here somewhere, Lou.

MARK. (*rushes behind counter*) I'll get a bucket of water!

LOU. Where, Darlene?

BARBIE JO. (*from kitchen*) Darlene, I need the fire extinguisher! Now!

DARLENE. (*getting upset*) Quit yellin' at me!

LOU. *(stops to comfort* **DARLENE***)* Darlene, honey, relax. Pretend it's just another fire drill! Take a deep breath. Now, think. Where's the extinguisher?

DARLENE. You know I don't do well under pressure, Lou!

*(***BOB*** crosses behind counter, lifts extinguisher right where* **MARK** *is filling the bucket with water, and hands the extinguisher to* **BARBIE JO** *through the kitchen window.)*

BOB. Here's the extinguisher, Barbie Jo. Need a hand?

MARK. I got a half bucket of water!

BARBIE JO. *(waves her hand about and coughs)* Thanks boys. It's not bad. Mostly just smoke.

BOB. *(coughs, fanning smoke away from his face)* I see that.

*(***MARK*** leans exhausted on the counter as* **BARBIE JO** *comes out of the kitchen holding another burned pie.)*

BARBIE JO. I didn't feel like drivin' to Springfield today anyhow. I'll send 'em a check. Let 'em buy their own pies!

LOU. It could save lives!

DARLENE. And whipped cream!

(During the chaos of the burning pies, **MARY SUE** *has disappeared from the restaurant. She is gone.)*

MARK. *(leaning on counter)* She's gone!

DARLENE. Who?

MARK. Mary Sue!

LOU. Mary Sue! She can't be gone! Where'd she go?

DARLENE. Her bag's gone!

*(***LOU*** grabs* **MARK** *from behind the counter and pushes him toward the front door.)*

LOU. Better get after her, Mark! She'll get lost in this snow storm for sure!

MARK. *(nods as he pulls on his hat)* Yes, Miss Lou. Should I bring her back here?

LOU. I'll be open as long as Bob's here. As long as there's a customer in the place, the diner's always open.

MARK. I'll be right back!

*(**MARK** exits front door.)*

LOU. I'm callin' Bill.

(reaches for her cell phone and dials)

He's the best tracker in town! Those boys have had plenty of time to blow off their macho steam. It's time they come home and act like adults!

BARBIE JO. Amen!

LOU. Mark's gonna need help if he doesn't find that girl quick!

DARLENE. *(totally breaks down)* Lou, you don't think she'll get lost, do ya? I mean, really lost?

BARBIE JO. *(shakes her head in disbelief)* Have you looked outside, Darlene?

LOU. *(looks out front window, puzzled)* For once, Darlene, I'm not sure what to think.

MARY, MARY – **LOU, BARBIE JO, & DARLENE**

LOU.

MARY, MARY IT IS TRUE.
YOU HAVE OH, SO MUCH TO DO.
MARY, MARY NEED I SAY,
THINGS HAVE ALWAYS BEEN THAT WAY.

IN THE MORNING, IN THE EVENING
YOU WILL CLIMB A MOUNTAIN HIGH
IN THE QUIET OF THE DAWNING
YOU WILL HEAR A BABY'S CRY

LOU & BARBIE JO.

MARY, MARY IT IS TRUE.
YOU HAVE OH, SO MUCH TO DO.
MARY, MARY NEED I SAY,
THINGS HAVE ALWAYS BEEN THAT WAY.

BARBIE JO.

IN THE COMING, IN THE GOING
WHEN THE STORM BEGINS TO BLOW
YOU WILL SENSE A MOTHER'S CALLING
YOU WILL KNOW WHICH WAY TO GO

ALL.

>MARY, MARY IT IS TRUE.
>YOU HAVE OH, SO MUCH TO DO.
>MARY, MARY NEED I SAY,
>THINGS HAVE ALWAYS BEEN THAT WAY.

DARLENE.

>IN THE HOPING, IN THE HEALING
>LEAN ON GOD HE IS YOUR FRIEND
>IN THE BRILLIANT STARLIGHT TWINKLING
>YOU WILL SEE YOUR STRUGGLE END

ALL.

>MARY, MARY IT IS TRUE.
>YOU HAVE OH, SO MUCH TO DO.
>MARY, MARY NEED I SAY,
>THINGS HAVE ALWAYS BEEN THAT WAY.

>*(Action in diner freezes as* **BOB** *speaks to the audience.)*

BOB/NARRATOR. We were all worried about Mary Sue. I kept hopin' Mark'd find her and bring her right back, but as the minutes dragged on, an unhappy gloom settled over the diner and all of us inside. The weather'd taken a definite turn for the worse, and the wind was makin' that mournful howlin' noise it makes when a real blizzard sets in. Never cared much for that sound. It always seemed like a bad omen. I couldn't stop thinkin' 'bout that poor girl, alone in the storm. I had a bad feelin'. A real bad feelin' that just kept gettin' worse and worse.

>*(curtain)*

ACT II

Scene One

*(The woods. Heavy snow falling. Wind whips the snow along center stage. **MARY SUE** can barely see through the storm as she fumbles along using the trees to support herself. She heads downstage left from upstage right. She is lost. Her hand flies to her stomach as she realizes that she has gone into labor. [As the scene unfolds, the restaurant set is transformed into the Wilson's shed. The set change is helped along as **BOB/NARRATOR** and the girls leave the stage. The swirly snow and sound of wind helps the set change. If the play is being done as a Two Act play, set change can be done during intermission.] **MARK** suddenly appears like a snowman, covered head to foot in snow.)*

*(**MARK** calls out to be heard over the storm. Searches the woods for **MARY SUE** urgently.)*

MARK. Mary Sue! Mary Sue! Where are you?

*(**MARY SUE** moans in agony. **MARK** hears and gets closer to her, still searching.)*

Mary Sue! Is that you? Where are you, Mary Sue?

MARY SUE. Mark?

MARK. Mary Sue, why'd you run away? I gotta take you back right now!

MARY SUE. Mark, why are you following me? I'm fine! Leave me be!

MARK. No you're not! You can't be out in this storm in your condition!

MARY SUE. I'm fine. Reall…Oh, God! What's that?

(looks down at herself)

MARK. What's what?

MARY SUE. I think my water just broke! The baby's coming! Oh, Mark! Help me!

MARK. We can't go back now! It's too far!

(yelling over the storm)

We've got to find shelter! You're nearly frozen as it is! There's an old cabin up here somewhere. Maybe we can find that.

MARY SUE. Are you sure, Mark? Because I don't think I can walk much farther!

(pause)

Oh, a contraction!

MARK. *(frustrated and frantic)* I'm sure the cabin's here somewhere. I can't see in this snow! Which way is north!

MARY SUE. Don't ask me! Owwww!

MARK. My pa came up here to stitch up a Mr. Miller's hand. He'd caught it in some barbed wire. Needed a tetanus shot and everything.

*(**MARY SUE** moans in pain again.)*

Course, that was a while back. I don't know where anything is, and...

MARY SUE. Mark, help me, please! It hurts!

MARK. Oh, God! That's not good!

MARY SUE. Why didn't I stay in town?

MARK. *(supports **MARY SUE**)* Come on. Easy now. Easy now, Mary Sue. Everything's fine. We're gonna be just fine!

MARY SUE. I hope so, Mark. I really hope so!

MARK. You...you lean on me! We'll find shelter somehow!

(to himself)

God, show me the way.

*(Bewildered, **MARK** helps **MARY SUE** as they start off into the storm. Lights cross-fade to Scene Five.)*

Scene 2

(Interior hunting cabin. The hunters return. **JIMMY** *turns as he enters to see* **DAVE** *following him into the cabin.* **BILL** *enters last.)*

JIMMY. Good grief, Dave! You scared me to death! You look like Sasquatch!

*(***DAVE*** enters looking like a snowman – covered head to toe by the blasting snow.* **JIMMY** *pulls off his hat and throws it on the bar.)*

DAVE. And you look like Frosty the Redneck Snowman! Let me in so I can get some circulation back in my feet!

(They continue stomping their feet and shaking off the snow as they talk.)

BILL. Listen, boys, that's no ordinary snow storm out there. I saw sandstorms in the gulf that weren't this bad!

JIMMY. What?!

DAVE. You tryin' to scare Jimmy? Cuz it's working.

BILL. Listen, Dave – if you want to hide from your monster-in-law, go back and do it in the hideout! We have to get off this mountain now, or we could be stuck here for weeks!

DAVE. You're probably right. Besides, I miss Barbie Jo and the kids. Maybe I should forget about putting my foot down. I can always be a man next year.

JIMMY. Snow wimp!

DAVE. Did I tell you the hideout has all the comforts of home? Bedroom, living room, kitchen…

JIMMY. And indoor plumbin'!

DAVE. Microwave too! Picked it up at Stan's garage sale last week!

JIMMY. Who could ask for more? Let's go!

*(***BILL*** checks cell phone.)*

BILL. Wait a minute! I got a message on my phone. It's from Lou. She says the storm's a blizzard. Roads in town are blowin' closed. We're leavin' now! Pack up!

DAVE. Call Lou and tell her we're on our way!

BILL. I can't get a signal. The storm's cut reception.

(**BILL** and **JIMMY** *frantically start packing up while* **DAVE** *heads out to the truck.*)

DAVE. I'll go put the rifles in the truck and get her warmed up.

(**DAVE** *exits.*)

JIMMY. *(hollering after* **DAVE***)* That truck's probably the only thing you're gonna warm up tonight! Barbie Jo's gonna be so mad when you get home, you'll be lucky if she let's you near her or the kids!

BILL. Yeah, well, let that be a lesson to you, Jimmy. That's what happens when you settle down.

JIMMY. *(picks up empty cans and tosses them into the cooler)* Heck, I know that! That's why you don't see a ring through this man's nose. Darlene's been chasing this hunk of country ham since we met on Clod Hoppers. com.

BILL. Who'd have thought you'd find a local girl on that thing?

JIMMY. Meant to be, Bill. Course, a hog farmer couldn't do no better than finding a girl on the internet! If'n they know computers, you know you got one with brains! Once I saw her picture, I knew Darlene was the girl for me!

(discovers half-full can and drinks it down)

Course that don't mean I'm ready to give up playing the field jes' yet.

BILL. *(stuffing gear into his duffel)* Yeah, but the field isn't giving you as much playing time as it used to, old buddy. You may want to reconsider Darlene before you're all played out and she's ready to trade you in for a rookie!

JIMMY. What, trade in Jimmy the Love God! Darlene wouldn't do that? We have an understanding. She knows how I feel. We don't need some piece of paper to tell us we're a couple!

(looking around)

JIMMY. *(lcont.)* Where the heck's my other hat?

BILL. *(flips* **JIMMY** *a large beaver cap)* One thing I've learned from twenty years of marriage is women love that piece of paper. They love the officialness, the permanence. Think of it like having the pink slip on your truck! That's how women feel about a marriage license. Once they have it, they have that extra 'pride of ownership'!

JIMMY. You make me sound like a '68 Camaro!

BILL. More like a '74 Gremlin! With a draggin' tailpipe.

JIMMY. *(puts his ridiculous fur cap on his head with great pride)* Well, Darlene's just fine with the way things are.

BILL. Lou Lou told me more than once that you're gonna lose Darlene if you don't make a real commitment, and I mean soon!

JIMMY. *(looks horrified)* Commitment! Sounds so final!

DAVE. *(enters angry)* Jimbo! When you checked the weather earlier, did you think about turning off the ignition when you finished?

JIMMY. *(distracted)* Huh?

DAVE. You left the key on, you idiot! The battery's dead. We're stuck here, you dope! How could this happen!

*(***BILL** *and* **DAVE** *look at* **JIMMY** *who sheepishly looks away.)*

And you better not pout.

JIMMY. And you better not shout!

DAVE. Why?

BILL. I'm tellin' you why!

JIMMY & DAVE. Why?

BILL. Because we're about to freeze to death! That's why!

DAVE. We can always feed Jimmy more of that chili and use him as a source of renewable fuel!

BILL. *(paces)* Don't stand there crackin' jokes! I'll try my cell phone again. Check yours for a signal!

DAVE. I can't believe I'm missing Christmas Eve dinner with my family!

JIMMY. Seems to me that's why you took us on this trip in the first place? Mr. "I got my own *macho...man...masculine...testosterone-filled* hideout"!

BILL. *(checks phone)* No signal yet! Listen, if we can't get back to town, we'll have to find some wood. Charlie Wilson has that old livestock shed about a mile back. There may be firewood there. If not, we can take a few slats off the shed and burn 'em to keep warm. We'll fix it later.

DAVE. You sure Charlie's cows won't mind a little draft up their udders?

JIMMY. *(sarcastically)* Maybe if it's cold enough we can get some ice cream from them cows for Christmas Eve dinner!

DAVE. *(not amused)* I can't believe I won't be with Barbie Jo and the kids on Christmas Eve. We could freeze to death! Why'd I do this? God is punishing me for being stupid!

BILL. If God punished you every time you were stupid, Dave, He wouldn't have time for nothin' else!

JIMMY. Well, at least I know who to blame for wrecking my Christmas Eve date with Darlene.

(takes out his cell phone and starts punching in numbers)

BILL. Jimmy, you only think you have a date with Darlene! Did you even get her a present?

JIMMY. Well...not exactly. But Darlene don't need gifts. She loves me for me, not what I buy her!

DAVE. Darlene may love the cupcake, but believe me, she's a woman, and women ain't happy unless the cupcake's got a nice thick layer of icing!

JIMMY. *(trying his phone)* Deader than a doornail! So much for that fancy four gee network and their big impressive map!

(frantically pushes buttons, reaches up to try to get a signal, knocks phone on the table)

DAVE. *(panicking)* You guys don't understand! We have to get home! My kids need me!

BILL. Pull yourself together, Dave. Service is down until the storm blows itself out. We'll get some wood for now and wait for a signal. Then we call for help. Simple. Just stay calm. You don't see Jimmy and me falling apart, do you!

(JIMMY *is panicked, punching buttons and smashing phone on the table.)*

WE ARE MEN! - JIMMY, DAVE, AND BILL

JIMMY.

NO MEAT FOR A MEAL,

DAVE.

NO FUEL FOR A FIRE,

JIMMY.

NO THERMOSTAT HERE
TO PUSH HIGHER AND HIGHER.

DAVE.

NO MODERN DAY COMFORTS,

JIMMY.

NO SLICK CONVERSATION,

DAVE.

NO HUMMER OR JEEP
GIVING QUICK TRANSPORTATION.

JIMMY.

OH WHAT WILL WE DO
OUT HERE IN THE COLD?

DAVE.

WHAT IF WE DIE
BEFORE WE GROW OLD?

BILL.

>WE ARE MEN!
>WE'LL SURVIVE!
>WE'LL FORAGE AND FEND,
>WE'LL MANAGE SOMEHOW!
>WE ARE MEN!

JIMMY.

>NO SHELTER,
>NO BLANKETS TO SPREAD ON THE BED,

DAVE.

>NOTHING FOR REAL MEN
>TO EAT AND BE FED.

JIMMY.

>NO SNACKS HERE BEYOND
>A FEW BEERS AND SOME NUTS

DAVE.

>THIS CHRISTMAS IS REALLY
>KICKING MY BUTT!

JIMMY.

>NO FEMININE COMFORT,
>NO SWEET HAND TO HOLD,

DAVE.

>AS WE ALL SADDLE UP
>TO FACE DOWN THE COLD.

JIMMY.

>OH, WHAT IF WE DIE
>BEFORE WE GROW OLD?

DAVE.

>OH, WHAT IF WE DIE
>BEFORE WE GROW OLD?

BILL.

>WE ARE MEN!
>WE'LL SURVIVE!
>WE'LL FORAGE AND FEND,
>WE'LL MANAGE SOMEHOW!
>WE ARE MEN!

DAVE.

    NO FAST FUEL INJECTION

JIMMY.

    NO GREEN COLEMAN GEAR

DAVE.

    NO SHELTERED PROTECTION
    BEYOND WHAT IS HERE.

JIMMY.

    WE'RE ALL BEYOND HOPE.

DAVE.

    I SEE NO WAY OUT!

JIMMY.

    WE'RE ALL GONNA DIE.

DAVE.

    OF THAT THERE'S NO DOUBT!

BILL.

    WE ARE MEN!
    WE'LL SURVIVE!
    WE'LL FORAGE AND FEND,
    WE'LL MANAGE SOMEHOW!
    WE ARE MEN!

JIMMY.

    I'LL WRITE MY LAST WILL.

DAVE.

    I'LL SAY MY GOODBYES.

JIMMY.

    OH HOW COULD IT END
    OUT HERE WITH YOU GUYS?

DAVE.

    NO HOPE FOR REDEMPTION

JIMMY.

    NO LAST MISTLETOE

DAVE.

    NO MORE TAX EXEMPTIONS!

JIMMY.

    MY HEART'S FILLED WITH WOE

DAVE. *(speaks)* Woe?

JIMMY.
> IT RHYMED.

DAVE.
> BUT WOE?

JIMMY.
> JUST CUZ I'M A HOG FARMER, DON'T MEAN I AIN'T SMART!

BILL. *(aside)*
> WE ARE MEN!
> WE ARE STRONG!
> AND WE'RE RIGHT TO THE END!
> DON'T LISTEN TO THEM!
> WE ARE MEN!

> WE ARE MEN!
> WE'LL SURVIVE!
> WE'LL FORAGE AND FEND,
> WE'LL MANAGE SOMEHOW!
> WE ARE MEN!

ALL.
> WE ARE MEN!
> WE'LL SURVIVE!
> WE'LL FORAGE AND FEND,
> WE'LL MANAGE SOMEHOW!
> WE ARE MEN!

DAVE. That's it! I'm walking back to town. If I leave my stuff here, I can hike to town. It's not far.

BILL. Not far. Just dangerous. Be sensible! The snow's filled in deep ravines and covered sharp rock formations. You've hunted these mountains all your life, but you won't recognize 'em now.

JIMMY. Bill's right! You're talkin' crazy, Dave! You'll be a human popsicle before you get to Grainger's Gulch.

BILL. We have to stick together. The only thing we can do is to get to Wilson's shed and get that fire wood. Remember, we are men!

DAVE. Okay. Okay.

BILL. Keep saying it. We are men. We are men.

DAVE. *(uncertainly)* We are men. If you say so, Bill.

BILL. I say so.

DAVE. We are men. We are men...

> *(The three men all have on crazy looking hunting hats as they exit the cabin and lights cross-fade to Scene Three.)*

Scene Three

(The Wilson's animal shed. Snow occasionally swirls between the slats in the rickety building. An old lantern is illuminated on a wooden box turned up on end. Bridles and lead ropes hang on the wall near the door. A chest which holds blankets, etc. sits beneath them. There are three stalls, and a door which leads to a small closet is stage right. A pile of loose wood lays near the door to the closet. MARK and MARY SUE stand just inside the closed door. She is in labor. If available, cows stand in the nearby stalls. MARK is worried, but tries to sound calm for MARY SUE.)

MARK. *(supports MARY SUE)* I have to get help, Mary Sue.

MARY SUE. Who?

MARK. I don't know. I can't leave you here alone, but we have to get help!

MARY SUE. There isn't time, Mark!

MARK. But you can't have a baby here, Mary Sue!

MARY SUE. I don't have a choice!

MARK. We can't get back to town! My cell phone isn't working. This is not good!

MARY SUE. Owww. Mark, do something. The baby's coming!

MARK. *(frantic)* Here? No! You can't have the baby here! Give me a minute to come up with something…

MARY SUE. When you figure it out, let me know, Mark! In the meantime, the baby's got other plans!

(MARY SUE goes into center stall and sits on hay. The stall door remains open)

MARK. No, Mary Sue! Don't sit down!

(She opens her coat.)

No, no! Don't open your coat!

(She props her legs firmly on the floor.)

No no! Mary Sue, don't make it easier! Not here!

(He joins **MARY SUE** *in center stall.)*

MARY SUE. *(groans)* Oww! Hold my hand, Mark – squeeze! Owwww!

(The front door flies opens – pushed in from outside. **JIMMY** *enters wearing his crazy hunting hat and a coat of snow. He looks in bewilderment at the scene in front of him.* **DAVE** *– wearing his own crazy hunting hat – runs into* **JIMMY** *stopped in the doorway.* **BILL** *runs into* **DAVE**. **DAVE** *and* **BILL** *do not see* **MARY SUE** *and* **MARK***.)*

DAVE. Why'd you stop? Get out of the way!

JIMMY. Uh fellas, we've got company.

BILL. What are you babbling about?

DAVE. Yeah, what? Wilson's cows playing 'Strip Poker'? Move, will ya?

MARK. *(approaches* **BILL***)* Mr. Wexler! Thank God you found us! I knew someone'd be looking for us!

BILL. Mark, what are you doing up here?

(motions to **MARY SUE***)*

Who on earth is that?

MARK. That's Mary Sue Archer. She's new in town. Just arrived today.

JIMMY. *(indicates* **MARK***)* Kid works fast!

MARK. It's a long story, Mr. Wexler.

BILL. Pleased to meet you, Mary Sue.

*(***BILL**, **DAVE**, & **JIMMY** *nod in her direction.* **MARY SUE** *nods back.)*

What in blazes are you two doing here in a blizzard?

*(***MARY SUE** *growls at him in pain.)*

OK, ma'am! Calm down. I'm sorry I asked.

MARK. There's no time to explain! She's about to have a baby!

DAVE, BILL, & JIMMY. Baby!

DAVE. This ain't no place to have a baby!

MARK. That's what I keep tellin' her!

JIMMY. Can't you find a cork and kinda stop her up for a while?

MARK. Is the truck outside? We could get to the hospital if we hurry!

BILL. Truck? The truck's got a dead battery! We're stuck here too!

MARY SUE. *(birth breathing)* I'm not feeling so good, Mark.

JIMMY. *(looking at* **MARY SUE***)* I don't feel so good neither. I'm headin' back to the cabin fellas. Childbirth ain't no place for a confirmed bachelor!

BILL. Stay right where you are! We need every able bodied man on this mission.

DAVE. Even you!

BILL. Besides, you see your hogs giving birth all the time. What's the problem? Maybe you should get in there and help that girl.

JIMMY. No way! If that baby don't come out with a curly tail and a snout, I won't know which end is up.

BILL. Pile up blankets and anything else you find. We'll need to bundle that baby up when it comes. Dave, check that chest by the wall! Jimmy, get in there and help that girl.

*(***DAVE*** *goes to chest and starts pulling out items.* ***JIMMY*** *stands looking at* ***MARY SUE*** *as she moans and groans.)*

JIMMY. How old you think she is, Bill?

BILL. Sixteen. Seventeen, maybe. Why?

JIMMY. Come on, Bill! Sixteen'll get me twenty! I ain't going nowhere near that!

BILL. Then tie those loose pieces of wood. Use those lead ropes and bridles. We'll make a sled. Take the blankets, put 'em on top, and we can drag Mary Sue and the baby back to the cabin.

JIMMY. Are you kidding?

BILL. Need my knife?

JIMMY. Hell no! Been huntin' since I was old enough to walk. Got my own knife.

(Checks his pockets. Knife is missing. Quietly, aside to **DAVE.***)*

Uh Dave, mind if I borrow your knife?

DAVE. *(holds up hoof pick)* How about this? Can you use this thing?

MARY SUE. *(groans)* Oh, Oh, it's coming!

BILL. Dave, do you know what that is? It's a hoof pick, you idiot! Unless you're gonna take it in there and clean her feet, I'd suggest you keep lookin'!

(to **MARK***)*

How close is she to delivering?

*(***MARY SUE** *groans louder than ever. She pants in a labored rhythm.)*

MARK. I think I heard her say, "It's coming," Mr. Wexler.

BILL. It's Bill! Just Bill!

(grabs **MARK** *and shoves him into stall)*

You help her, Mark. You're in med school!

DAVE. Here's a saddle. With stirrups!

JIMMY. Don't they use stirrups for birthin' babies?

BILL. Sure! Put her head on the saddle and her feet in the stirrups.

MARK. OK, Mr. Wexler. I'll try!

*(***BILL** *closes stall door to give* **MARY SUE** *privacy.)*

DAVE. *(still searching chest)* I found this.

(holds up small jar)

BILL. What is it?

DAVE. Bag balm!

(removes lid, smells ointment)

Smells good!

BILL. *(crosses to* **DAVE***)* What the hell's bag balm?

DAVE. I don't know! Jimmy's the farmer!

(to **JIMMY***)*

What's bag balm?

JIMMY. What makes you think I know? I take good care of my hogs, but I keep it purely professional! I don't get involved in their beauty treatments!

BILL. *(takes jar from* **DAVE***)* It says here...

(reading)

"Apply liberally to udders. Heals cracking. Soothes discomfort from chapping."

DAVE. *(takes jar back possessively)* Mary Sue! I know we just met and all, but are you by any chance plannin' to breast feed that baby?

*(**MARY SUE***'s voice comes from the stall harsh and angry)*

MARY SUE. Leave...me...alone! I'm...busy...in... here!

DAVE. *(to* **BILL***)* Do you think she's always like that?

JIMMY. *(scared by* **MARY SUE***'s voice)* This stress is affecting my bladder.

(starts to flee)

I'll be right back!

BILL. *(still at chest)* No you don't! Get that sled together! Doesn't sound like we have much time!

DAVE. *(digging in chest)* Saddle soap! Hey, this'll help him slip that baby right outta there! Mark, you think this saddle soap'll help?

MARY SUE. You come in here with that saddle soap, and you'll leave with it stuffed where the sun don't shine!

MARK. *(pops head up over stall door)* I'd say that's a 'no' Mr. Fox. Thanks anyhow.

(pops back down and out of sight)

DAVE. *(to* **BILL***)* Touchy! Don't you think?

BILL. That ain't nothin'. Wait 'til the head starts comin' out!

JIMMY. *(panicked and near to passing out)* Oh Lord! Oh Lord! The head.

(distracting himself)

Bill, there's some wood in that first stall. I'm gonna see if we can use it.

BILL. Just get to it!

JIMMY. *(enters first stall)* This big piece here in the corner looks good. Here! Praise the Lord!

(Pulls wood and rear corner of the stable falls in. A mound of snow falls into the corner on **JIMMY.***)*

BILL. That's just great, Jim! Mary Sue'd be better off outside!

JIMMY. *(stands there with a slim pole in his hand)* Quit yellin' at me! My delicate system's actin' up again!

BILL. *(Tensely. Picks up box from chest,)* Quit your whinin', and finish that sled. We can't have a baby in here with snow flyin'!

JIMMY. *(loud and angry)* Who do I look like? MacGyver! Why don't you do somethin' besides boss me around for a change?

DAVE. *(gets up with bag balm in his hand)* Would you two forget about who's doin' what and get movin'. That baby ain't gonna wait on us!

JIMMY. Who asked you? I don't see you doin' nothin' to help neither! Same as always. 'Jimmy, do this', 'Jimmy, do that'!

BILL. How about 'Jimmy, shut up'!

(Then from the quiet of the center stall, we hear a slap and a baby's cry. Lights soften. **BILL** *and the boys slowly come forward and opens the stall door. The scene is now lighted through a scrim in front of the stall so that the men are seen in silhouette – casting large shadows of "The Three Wise Men" on the wall.* **BILL** *is farthest from* **MARY SUE** *holding a box from the chest.* **JIMMY** *is next in line, holding the staff of wood.* **DAVE** *holds the jar of bag balm from the chest.)*

*(***MARY SUE*** *sits with a blue blanket pulled up over her shoulders sitting with her baby wrapped in small blankets. The visual effect is a recreation of the Virgin Mary at the Nativity.)*

*(***MARK*** *stands next to* ***MARY SUE*** *gazing at the mother and child. The saddle next to them is set up to give the appearance of a manger.* ***MARK*** *also has a blanket hanging long from his shoulders. His hand is on* ***MARY SUE'****s shoulder.* ***MARK*** *represents Joseph at the Nativity.)*

(A soft, musical version of Away in a Manger *plays softly in the background to set the mood for the sacred moment. The snowstorm abates. Stars shine through the windows. A spot is directed onto* ***MARY SUE*** *and the baby. This scene develops slowly and glorifies into the Nativity. A large star shines through the hole in the roof.)*

(Lights start to return to normal. Cast remains frozen, and a spot comes up on ***MARK*** *and the baby.* ***MARK*** *sings as the rest of the cast remain in tableau.)*

SNOWY CHRISTMAS DAY - MARK

MARK.

SNOW IS SOFTLY FALLING,
MIRACLES ARE CALLING,
BUT TONIGHT YOU'RE JUST A TINY BABE,
THEY CAN WAIT ANOTHER DAY.

YOUR MOMMA FACED THE DANGER,
PLACED YOU IN A MANGER,
TO HER YOU'RE SUCH A MIRACLE,
FOR US, YOU ARE THE WAY.

SEEMS I KNOW ANOTHER STORY STARTED JUST THIS WAY.
SEEMS ANOTHER MOTHER GOT DOWN ON HER KNEES TO
    PRAY.
SEEMS TO ME LIKE WAY BACK THEN, WE NEED SOME HELP
    TODAY.
SEEMS YOU MAKE THE DIFFERENCE ON THIS SNOWY
    CHRISTMAS DAY.

MARK. *(cont.)*

> NOT WHAT I IMAGINED,
> JUST A BIT OLD FASHIONED,
> OUT HERE IN THIS STABLE,
> WHILE THE SNOW KEEPS COMING DOWN.
>
> THESE THREE SURE AREN'T WISE MEN,
> THEY'RE NOT EVEN PRIZE MEN,
> BUT THEY WERE MEANT TO BE OUT HERE,
> INSTEAD OF BACK IN TOWN.
>
> SEEMS I KNOW ANOTHER STORY STARTED JUST THIS WAY.
> SEEMS ANOTHER MOTHER GOT DOWN ON HER KNEES TO
>   PRAY.
> SEEMS TO ME LIKE WAY BACK THEN, WE NEED SOME HELP
>   TODAY.
> SEEMS YOU MAKE THE DIFFERENCE ON THIS SNOWY
>   CHRISTMAS DAY.
>
> DID MY BEST TO HELP HER,
> HOPE I DIDN'T FALTER,
> SEEMED SHE NEEDED SOMEONE,
> WHO HAD A HAND TO HOLD.
>
> PROMISE TO STAND BY HER,
> BE A FRIEND AND GUIDE HER,
> JUST IN CASE THIS STORY'S
> LIKE ANOTHER TALE RETOLD.
>
> SEEMS I KNOW ANOTHER STORY STARTED JUST THIS WAY.
> SEEMS ANOTHER MOTHER GOT DOWN ON HER KNEES TO
>   PRAY.
> SEEMS TO ME LIKE WAY BACK THEN, WE NEED SOME HELP
>   TODAY.
> SEEMS YOU MAKE THE DIFFERENCE ON THIS SNOWY
>   CHRISTMAS DAY.

*(**MARK** returns to his place in the nativity, and spot goes dark.)*

Scene Four

(Everyone holds the tableau as the lights and music return to normal.)

BILL. *(clapping* **JIMMY** *on back)* Well, lookee there? We managed to get that baby born after all! I declare, we're pretty smart for three old country boys!

JIMMY. Yeah, well, we may be the wisest men in Dixie. But right now, I gotta take a leak!

(exits)

DAVE. Congratulations, Mary Sue! Is it a boy or a girl?

MARY SUE. A boy. Mark, isn't he beautiful!

(The loud sound of an air horn blasts. The entire shed rattles. Door opens with snow flying in. **LOU** *comes in with* **BARBIE JO** *and* **DARLENE**.*)*

BILL. *(closes the stall door to protect* **MARY SUE** *and the baby)* Hey, hey, hey, close that door! We got a babe in here!

BARBIE JO. Oh, really? Listen, Bill –

LOU. Barbie Jo, we agreed I'd handle this!

(to **BILL***)*

Okay, Bill. Start explaining! What are you doin' here in Charlie Wilson's shed?

*(**MARY SUE** giggles, cooing to the baby.* **LOU**, **DARLENE**, *and* **BARBIE JO** *cannot see into the stall as the door blocks their view.)*

MARY SUE. Aren't you just the sweetest, most adorable thing! Handsome too!

BARBIE JO. They do have a babe in here! Darlene, do you still carry that Derringer in your purse?

DARLENE. Sure, Barbie Jo. Why?

BARBIE JO. 'Cuz if Bill's here. And Dave's there. Then that's Jimmy in there ticklin' that babe's ivories!

DARLENE. *(horrified)* Jimmy wouldn't do that to me! I mean, we're practically married. He eats my cookin'! He's buying me a dog for Christmas! It can't be!

(calling toward center stall)

Jimmy Weaver, you in there?

BILL. Listen Lou – this is just a big misunderstanding.

LOU. You tellin' me that's NOT a girl makin' them sounds in there!

BILL. Technically… it is a girl, but we didn't bring her here.

BARBIE JO. *(to LOU)* How convenient. A giggly girl met up with them at Charlie Wilson's shed, where they weren't supposed to be in the first place! In the middle of a blizzard! On Christmas Eve!

DAVE. What made you come lookin' for us anyway? It's not like I'm not glad to see you. I mean, I am…

BARBIE JO. Mama was right! You are just a *man* after all!

DAVE. Your mama ain't never right! I ain't no man, and I can prove it!

DARLENE. Is that my Jimmy in there or not?

DAVE & BILL. Not!

DARLENE. Then where's Jimmy?

BILL. Outside takin' a leak!

DARLENE. Outside! Does he know how cold it is out there?

DAVE. I think he has an idea.

DARLENE. *(horrified, looks at audience)* I better get him in here quick! Can't have him getting frostbite!

(exits)

BARBIE JO. *(to DAVE)* This is the worst Christmas Eve of my entire life! I can never trust you again!

LOU. *(to DAVE)* Thanks for dragging Jimmy and Bill into your problems, Dave! Did you ever stop to think they should be home on Christmas Eve?

DAVE. *(turns to BILL)* Is that what you told her? That I dragged you along! You didn't even have the cajones to tell Lou you *wanted* to come up here today!

LOU. You wanted to get away too? Listen, Bill – just because we don't have kids, don't mean we aren't a family! Why would you want to get away on Christmas Eve?

BILL. Did you ever stop to think all the fussin' you do, about adopting a baby, makes me feel less of a man!

LOU. *(shocked)* What'd you say?

BILL. That's right! The one thing you have your heart set on – I can't give you! How do you think that makes me feel?

LOU. Well, I…I…

BILL. So when I ran into Dave and Jimmy at the VFW last night, we had a few drinks and started talkin' about hunting today. It seemed like the perfect opportunity to clear my head, that's all! It only took one day of insanity in the woods with these two to make me realize I'd made a huge mistake!

DAVE. Insanity! Hey, none of this was my fault! The only thing any of us managed to kill today was the battery in the truck! And I certainly can't be blamed for the blizzard! The whole thing is Mary Sue's fault!

BARBIE JO & LOU. Mary Sue!

(Suddenly the stall door opens, and MARY SUE steps out holding her baby. MARK supports her.)

MARY SUE. He's right, Miss Lou.

LOU. Mary Sue! What in tarnation…

MARY SUE. This is my son. Mr. Wexler, Mark, and the others helped! They all pitched in! I couldn't have done it without them. Your husbands really knew what to do.

DAVE. You see, Barbie Jo…your mother's all wrong about me. Fathering comes natural to me.

MARY SUE. Miss Lou, would you like to hold him?

(MARY SUE goes to LOU and puts the baby in her arms. LOU is now standing center stage holding the baby with BILL on one side and MARY SUE on the other. MARK stands behind MARY SUE admiring the baby over LOU's shoulder. BARBIE JO and DAVE stand off to one side.)

LOU. Well, I…

BILL. Go on, Lou Lou. Start practicing for when ours comes along.

LOU. I don't know what to say.

MARY SUE. Please, Miss Lou! Look, he's smiling!

LOU. Land's sake. He is!

BILL. I wonder if this little guy might be needin' a set of Godparents, Mary Sue. If you'd like, Lou and I'd be honored to help you raise this baby. Consider it our Christmas gift to you.

MARY SUE. You're so kind. But I can't accept any gifts.

(JIMMY and DARLENE enter, entwined in a passionate embrace. She leaves big lip prints on his face. BOB comes in behind them.)

I can't stay here. I don't have a job. I don't even have a place to live.

JIMMY. *(to LOU as he breaks from the clinch)* Couldn't help overhearing, Lou! Would it help if Darlene resigned because she didn't need her job anymore? Then Mary Sue could take her place at the diner!

BARBIE JO. Why on earth wouldn't Darlene need her job?

DARLENE. We're getting' married, Barbie Jo! Jimmy just asked me out in the snow! I'm gonna be a hog farmer!

DAVE. *(to JIMMY)* Meet her Mama first!

JIMMY. Mary Sue, you can work at the diner! Lou's place is the busiest restaurant in town!

MARY SUE. That's one problem solved, and with Lou and Bill to help take care of him…but, where would we live?

LOU. I haven't seen any apartments for rent since spring. Maybe we could convert our back bedroom, Bill.

BILL. It's awful small.

(pause)

Say how'd you gals know where to find us?

LOU. Stopped by Sheriff Bradley's office to use that GPS thing he has. He traced your cell phones. This was the only building close to the signal, so we checked here first!

(indicates **BOB***)*

Bob there drove us up!

BOB. My pleasure, ma'am. Wouldn't have missed this for the world.

DAVE. I was thinkin' maybe, since everyone else is giving out Christmas gifts, maybe Barbie Jo and I have something for Mary Sue too.

*(***BARBIE JO*** looks at* **DAVE***, perplexed.)*

BARBIE JO. What are you up to?

DAVE. I think you're gonna like this.

(to **MARY SUE***)*

Mary Sue, we have a cabin on our property. I've been fixin' it up the past few months. It's not much to look at, but it has all the comforts of home.

JIMMY. Even indoor plumbin'!

DAVE. It's completely insulated. Just finished installing it myself.

MARY SUE. If you've been fixin' it up, you must need it for something.

DAVE. Not really.

(hugs **BARBIE JO***)*

I need my family more.

(to **MARY SUE***)*

We'd be honored if you'd come live there – free of charge. Consider it a present from us – from all of your friends here in Christmas.

MARY SUE. *(emotional)* I don't know what I ever did to deserve such kindness. I can't imagine a better place to live than with the friends I've made here. Thank you. Thank you all!

DARLENE. *(to* **LOU***)* That's amazing! We just met Mary Sue a few hours ago. Now here she is, two people instead of one! Like a miracle!

(pause)

Think of it, Lou. A baby born in a stable on Christmas Eve. And our three boys here to witness the whole thing. Just like The Three…

LOU. Don't even think it!

BARBIE JO. Nah, that's too farfetched even for a Christmas miracle!

DARLENE. Oh Lord, I feel like singing again! Come on, Lou. Let's sing! Listen, the storm has stopped! I know!

(sings beautifully) Silent night, Holy night, All is calm, all is bright…

(All join **DARLENE** *as she sings and* **LOU** *rocks the baby.* **MARY SUE** *looks lovingly at her tiny son. Cast sings very quietly as* **BOB/NARRATOR** *steps forward to address audience. Cast will sing slowly once through* Silent Night, *and* **BOB/NARRATOR***'s monologue should end shortly before the song finishes.)*

BOB/NARRATOR. *(removes hat, scratching head)* Like I said. It really was a miracle. God certainly works in mysterious ways. We think we need one thing, but we really needed somethin' else all along. I've seen God send a lot of unusual answers to prayer, but nothin' like I saw here tonight!

(pause)

Them boys came through. That girl and her baby found a home and friends, and isn't that what Christmas is all about?

(indicating the scene behind him, more) Most folks think that first Christmas so long ago came off smooth as silk. Knowing human nature, I wonder if it wasn't more like my good old fashioned redneck country Christmas!

(pause)

BOB/NARRATOR. God bless, folks! Drive safe! And Merry Christmas!

(**BOB** *steps back in with the cast as the end* Silent Night, *and all join in for the last song!*)

A GOOD OLD FASHIONED REDNECK COUNTRY CHRISTMAS - ALL

BILL.

WE'LL HAVE A GOOD OLD FASHIONED REDNECK COUNTRY
CHRISTMAS.
LIKE THE HALLMARK CARDS YOU USED TO SEE.
WHILE SNOW KEEPS PILIN' HIGHER, WE'LL GATHER BY THE
FIRE.
STRINGIN' ALL THE LIGHTS UPON THE TREE.

DARLENE.

BAKE COOKIES WITH AUNT JOSEPHINE,
SHE'S THE CHRISTMAS COOKIE QUEEN, YOU KNOW.

JIMMY.

AND DON'T FORGET THE BEER!

BILL.

YOU WON'T WANT TO MISS THIS,
GOOD OLD FASHIONED REDNECK COUNTRY CHRISTMAS.

BARBIE JO.

BAKIN' UP THE PUMPKIN PIES
TO TAKE 'EM TO THE LOCAL CHARITY.
HELPIN' PREACHER ERNIE
WITH COSTUMES FOR THE CHURCH NATIVITY.
NO MATTER HOW YOU'RE LIVIN', SET YOUR HEART ON GIVIN'.
SHARE A SMILE WITH EVERYONE YOU SEE.
YOUR GIFTS WILL ALL COME BACK TO YOU, MORE AND MORE
AND MORE I GUARANTEE!

BOB.

WE'LL HAVE A GOOD OLD FASHIONED REDNECK COUNTRY
CHRISTMAS.
LIKE THE HALLMARK CARDS YOU USED TO SEE.
WHILE SNOW KEEPS PILIN' HIGHER, WE'LL GATHER BY THE FIRE.
STRINGIN' ALL THE LIGHTS UPON THE TREE.

LOU.

SING CAROLS WITH AUNT JENNIFER,
PLAYIN' ON THE WURLITZER, YOU KNOW.

BILL.

HEY, GRANDPA SHOT A DEER!

BOB.

YOU WON'T WANT TO MISS THIS,
GOOD OLD FASHIONED REDNECK COUNTRY CHRISTMAS.

DAVE.

I'M SICK OF ALL THE FAMILY FEUDS,
THE NAGGIN' AND THE ATTITUDES, IT'S TRUE.
CHRISTMAS WAS AN AWFUL CHORE,
AND LATELY NOT SO WHITE AS MUCH AS BLUE.

BILL.

BLUE CHRISTMAS.

DAVE.

IF YOU'RE SICK OF ALL THE NOISE, COME UP HERE WITH
JUST THE BOYS.
AVOID THE CONFLICT WITH YOUR FAMILY!
WE KNOW HOW TO CELEBRATE
CHRISTMAS AS IT'S ALWAYS MEANT TO BE!

ALL.

WE'LL HAVE A GOOD OLD FASHIONED REDNECK COUNTRY
CHRISTMAS!
LIKE THE HALLMARK CARDS YOU USED TO SEE.
WHILE SNOW KEEPS PILIN' HIGHER, WE'LL GATHER BY THE
FIRE.
STRINGIN' AND A SINGIN' 'ROUND THE TREE.

LOU.

STAYIN' OUT WITH UNCLE JOE,
MAKIN' ANGELS IN THE SNOW, YOU SEE!

DARLENE.

HOT CHOCOLATE'S JUST INSIDE!

ALL.

YOU WON'T WANT TO MISS THIS,
GOOD OLD FASHIONED REDNECK COUNTRY CHRISTMAS!
YOU WON'T WANT TO MISS THIS,
GOOD OLD FASHIONED REDNECK COUNTRY CHRISTMAS!

(curtain)

PROPS

Bakery box tied with string
Paper bag with handles
Wall Phone
Cell Phones (4)
Coffee Urn
Coffee Cup (2)
Saucer (2)
Silverware
Napkins
Menus
Scorched Pie (2)
Spray Can of Whipping Cream
Bell
Pocket Knife
Fire Extinguisher
Plates
Hunting Hats (3)
Split Logs
Canned Beverages
Empty Cans
Igloo Cooler
Slim Jims
Pork Rinds (bag)
Snow
Books
Notebooks
Pencils
Backpack
Satchel
Pregnancy Belly
Chest
Wooden Box
Old Lantern
Horse Blankets
Hoof Pick
Jar of Bag Balm
Bar of Saddle Soap
Baby doll (toy)
Wood Pieces

NOTE: It is my hope that actors and directors will add numerous 'Redneck' props and costume touches to this production list, enjoying the country setting as well as the country lifestyle. Have a good, old fashioned country good time!

– *KLB*

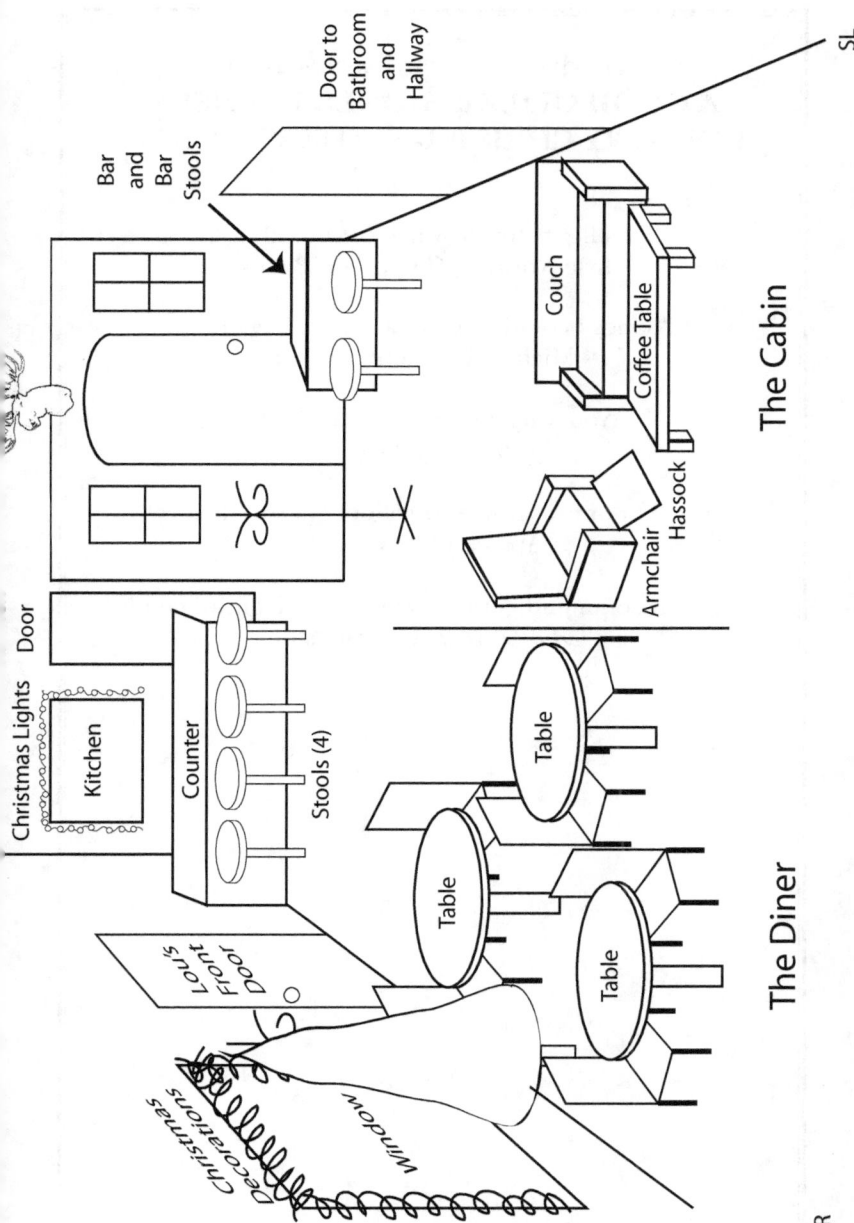

Door to
Bathroom
and
Hallway

Bar
and
Bar
Stools

Couch

Coffee Table

The Cabin

Armchair   Hassock

SL

Christmas Lights   Door

Kitchen

Counter

Stools (4)

LOU'S
FRONT
DOOR

Table

Table

Table

Table

The Diner

Christmas
Decorations

Window

SR

See what people are saying about
**A GOOD OLD FASHIONED REDNECK
COUNTRY CHRISTMAS: THE MUSICAL...**

"Excellent score! Worthy of Broadway!"
– Kyle Norman, Composer/Pianist

"Songs I could listen to again and again!"
– Michael Reimann, Author

"You will laugh and be touched."
– *Indianapolis Star*

"The first time a show ever sold out at this theatre!"
– Westfield Playhouse

"Highly recommend getting tickets for the entire family."
– *RedPub Magazine,* Houston

AVAILABLE FROM BAKER'S PLAYS

A GOOD OLD FASHIONED REDNECK COUNTRY CHRISTMAS

Kris Bauske

Comedy / 5m, 4f

Also available from Samuel French's subsidiary, Baker's Plays, non-musical version of A GOOD OLD FASHIONED REDNECK COUNTRY CHRISTMAS!

Lou's Diner is the friendliest place in the south, but this Christmas Eve, Lou and the girls are steamed. Lou's husband, Bill, and his pals Dave and Jimmy have taken off for a day of hunting in the mountains. Dave is married to one of Lou's waitresses while Jimmy is trying to avoid marriage to the other.

When Mary Sue, the pregnant and poignant stranger gets lost in the woods and ends up having her baby in a cow shed in the middle of a blizzard, the red-neck boys become the most unlikely Wise Men at the Nativity you ever saw! Bob is there to witness it all and give us the narrative of their adventure. The first miracle of Christmas blesses everyone in this tender comedy, and with simplicity and grace, gently reminds the audience of the real reason for the season!

Blending a healthy dollop of southern comedy with a pinch of O'Henry's *Gift of the Magi*, *A Good, Old Fashioned, Redneck Country Christmas* is overflowing with infectious high spirits! Laughs abound!

"Good, old fashioned entertainment for the entire family."
– Ken Eulo, Broadway Writer/Producer/Director

"Absolutely charming, delightful and entertaining. A funny, sensitive, gentle, highly respectful retelling of the greatest story ever told and well worth seeing again and again."
– Gersh Morningstar, *The Florida Blue Sheet*

OTHER TITLES AVAILABLE FROM SAMUEL FRENCH

A 1940'S RADIO CHRISTMAS CAROL

Walton Jones, David Wohl and Faye Greenberg

Musical Comedy / 6m, 3f, 2 optional characters for larger casts

The long-awaited sequel to the popular *The 1940's Radio Hour*. It's Christmas Eve, 1943, and the Feddington Players are now broadcasting from a hole-in-the-wall studio in Newark, NJ, and set to present their contemporary "take" on Dickens's A *Christmas Carol.* Whether it's the noisy plumbing, missed cues, electrical blackouts, or the over-the-top theatrics of veteran actor, but radio novice, William St. Claire, this radio show is an entertaining excursion into the mayhem and madness of a live radio show. St. Claire's escalating foibles and acting missteps propel the show to a simultaneously comedic and heart-wrenching dramatic climax: St. Claire has an on-air breakdown, and begins to connect his own life with that of the classic Dickens tale. In order to "save the show," the company improvises an ending to Charles Dickens' classic as a film noir mystery, featuring a hardboiled detective, a femme fatale, and an absurd rescue of Tiny Tim (and the Lindbergh baby) from the clutches of a Hitler-esque villain named Rudolf! High School Musical lyricist Faye Greenberg and composer David Wohl have written four delightful period songs for the Feddington Players, and swing arrangements of many Christmas standards. Seamlessly combining drama and comedy, heartbreak and hope, *The 1940's Radio Christmas Carol* will sing its way into your heart. If you enjoyed 1940's Radio Hour, step back in time once again with the Feddington Players, and get into the holiday spirit with *The 1940's Radio Christmas Carol.*

"A reading that transforms Charles Dickens's classic into a gumshoe mystery...far above the usual holiday offerings."
– Stacy Nick, *Coloradoan*